With a billion people going to bed hungry, how is it ok that we waste food?

It's time for change. Here's how...

Contents

Introduction   6

The history of food waste   11
Learning from the past   12
Factory farming   15
New farm machinery   18
Larger farms   19
Agronomy – agricultural research   21
The age of abundance and invisibility of food waste   21
Quality standards   22
A new century and a new awareness   23
Landfill tax   24
European Union legislation changes   24
Increasing food prices   25
Campaigns, activists and social media   25
Relaxation of some cosmetic standards for food   26
Increased consumer awareness   27
Increased visibility of food waste   29

Why do we waste so much of our food?   31
Aesthetics   32
Habit   34
Issues with portion size   36
Lack of planning   38
Too much information?   40
Misconceptions/misunderstandings   41
'Use by' and 'confuse by' dates   42

Making the most of our food   45
The nose to tail approach   47
Better food storage   47
Temperature guidelines for high risk foods   48
Other food storage guidelines   49
Fridge management   50
Fridge temperature   51
Fridge organisation   51
Stock rotation   52
Food banks and food sharing   54
Food sharing apps   57
Gleaning and abundance groups   58
What we really can't eat and why   59

Leftover Pie

*

101 ways to reduce
your food waste

Written by
Anna Pitt

For my Mum, who loved food a lot.

Published by: Green Lanes Publishing

Copyright © Anna Pitt 2017

ISBN: 978-0-9574637-1-4

Growing your own 61
Herbs 62
Vegetables 71

What should we do with our unavoidable food waste? 75
Animal feed – The Pig Idea 76
Anaerobic digestion 81
Composting 86
Bokashi 89
Wormeries 91

What if we just throw it all in the bin? 97
Energy from waste using incineration (burning) 98
Landfill 99
Leachate 99
Greenhouse gases 100
What if you don't have a separate food waste collection
    and don't have room to compost at home? 101

The future of food 103
More plant, less meat 104
Localism and seasonal eating 106
Vertical/urban farming 107
Insect protein 108
Closing the loop on waste 109

101 Great Waste Busting Recipes

Making the most of your meat 115
Making the most of your vegetables 125
Using up the glut from the garden and hedgerows 137
Loving your leftovers 151
Better use of the bits 163
Use-it-up snacks and light lunches 177
Soups and sauces 187
Cakes and desserts 201
Store cupboard meals 213
About the contributors 219
Acknowledgements 228
About the author 230
Index of recipes 231

Introduction

In 2013, I took part in Zero Waste Week which, that year, was helping people reduce their food waste. I was fairly confident that I was good at making the most of my food and was very aware of the extent of the food waste problem, having devoted the first chapter of my book, *101 Ways to Live Cleaner and Greener for Free*, to this. I was giving talks in primary and secondary schools around the UK, campaigning to get children and young people to rethink their attitude towards waste, encouraging them to persuade their parents that they needed to look at their food habits as part of this.

But I had never thought to measure and monitor my own food waste. So, I pledged to do exactly that during Zero Waste Week and to blog about my findings on a daily basis. It was enlightening and got me visiting parts of my fridge I hadn't seen in a long while. It made me realise that I was still a big part of the problem, even though I was trying hard to be part of the solution.

2014 was designated the European Year Against Food Waste. So why did we need a year devoted to reducing food waste and has it helped?

In 2012, the European Parliament wrote:

"Every year in Europe a growing amount of healthy, edible food – some estimates say up to 50% – is lost along the entire food supply chain, in some cases all the way up to the consumer, and becomes waste."[1]

This illustrates that food waste is a huge problem. It seems incredible that almost half the food that is produced in Europe goes to waste. Many people think the food

1 European Parliament resolution of 19 January 2012 on how to avoid food wastage: strategies for a more efficient food chain in the EU

waste problem is outside of their control. They believe the problem lies in the supply chain, or it's the fault of the weather, or the supermarkets, or the hospitality industry. They don't believe they are part of the problem.

"Yes, it is us!
It is you and me."

We are wasting food in our own homes. Food that we have paid for with our hard-earned cash; food that we have spent time buying; food we have taken the time to prepare. That's our time, our money and yes, it is within our control.

In 2015, household waste stood at 7.3 million tonnes.[2] That's around a quarter of all the food and drink that we buy. Fortunately, these food waste figures are heading in the right direction; the previous annual waste figure from 2007 was 8.3 million tonnes.[3]

There has been a huge increase in awareness of food waste; we see the issue on national television; supermarkets make regular announcements showing they are putting surplus food to good use; food surplus cafés are popping-up; and organisations such as The Gleaning Network, Feeding the 5000, and FareShare are no longer just talked about by waste worriers like me.

Yet food waste is still happening by the millions of tonnes and where once people were very quick to blame supermarkets, it is now becoming clear that 50% of our wasted food is wasted by people at home. This is good to

2 www.wrap.org.uk/content/household-food-waste-uk-2015-0
3 www.wrap.org.uk/content/estimates-household-food-and-drink-waste-uk-2011

know, because it means that we can become a part of the solution.

When I first started researching this book I thought I'd look back at my food waste from day one of Zero Waste Week 2013.

Here's the list:

- Two banana skins
- The outer peel from four onions
- Four teabags
- The skin from half a squash
- The ends chopped off some green beans.

It weighed 524 grammes. I think most of the weight was in the squash skin and I really did try to scrape every bit of flesh from it.

This equates to 191,391 grammes per year.

In 2015, there were 27 million households in the UK. Assuming every household produces a similar amount of food waste to me, then we'd have an annual food waste figure of 5,164,020 tonnes. Remember, though, I didn't throw away any squishy cucumbers or wilting lettuce. We ate the mushy bananas from the speckled brown jackets and just had the skins left over.

So that figure of 7.3 million tonnes suggests some households eat a lot of squash or there's a lot of food being thrown away that could have been eaten.

In fact, the Waste and Resources Action Programme (WRAP) reports that of the 7.3 million tonnes of household food and drink wasted, we could have eaten or drunk 4.2

million tonnes of it.[4] So, it's not all about banana skins, tea bags and squash peel, which most people currently consider to be unavoidable waste.

What's more WRAP tells us that it is costing us around £12.5 billion. With so many families in the UK feeling the effects of austerity, this is clearly unsustainable.

While in the UK and many other countries we are wasting all this food, one in eight people on this planet go to bed hungry. How can that be? What is going wrong in our global food system?

Let's start by asking why we are wasting all that food. Do we need to look at our food habits and find out what lies behind that wasted £12.5 billion? Do we need to rethink our global food economy to make sure that everyone on this planet gets their fair share?

When my grandmother read my first book, *101 Ways to Live Cleaner and Greener for Free*, she said:

"Do you know what I think, Anna? I think a big part of the problem is down to my generation. I think my generation, having lived through the war, got so fed up of having nothing and needing to scrimp and save and eke out our rations, that when things became more plentiful we became wasteful."

That made me think about the history of food waste and how it has shaped our eating and throwing away habits. So, in the first chapter of this book, we look at food waste over the last 100 years to work out how we got to where we are today, which I call a 'food waste crisis point'.

---

4 WRAP 'Household Food Waste Report 2015' at www.wrap.org.uk/content/household-food-waste-uk-2015-0 .

The second chapter considers why we waste so much of our food. In the third chapter, we look at how we can make the most of our food.

The fourth chapter deals with what happens to our food waste and how we can improve the way we deal with it. Chapter five looks at the problems people are causing if they don't deal with their food waste in the right way, and in the sixth chapter, we look at the future of food and think about ways we could change and diversify our diets to ensure that we can feed the nine billion people we expect to have on our planet by the year 2050.

Then, there are 101 great recipes. The recipes in this book are a combination of family favourites that have helped us reduce the amount of food we waste, and waste-saving favourites of top chefs, food writers, and campaigners around the UK.

I hope you find something in this book to inspire you to make more of your food. Food is a precious and wonderful thing.

The history of food waste

Learning from the past

When we want to find out why we do something, it sometimes helps to look back and see how our customs and habits have changed over the years. How does the amount of food we waste compare with the food our great grandparents' generation wasted?

I asked my grandmother, who was born in 1921, to tell me about how they shopped, cooked and dealt with food waste when she was a child.

They didn't have supermarkets, so they would buy their meat from the butcher, their groceries (flour, salt and sugar) from the grocer and much of their fruit and veg was grown by her dad in their garden. Food was generally local and seasonal.

She remembers collecting food waste for her Uncle George to make feed for his pigs. What surprised me was that she mentioned bread crusts as food waste. I always use up my bread crusts, but I have long been the recipient of her crusts, some of which I've used in stuffing or for toast, but they've always been given to me for 'the animals' – my elderly pony particularly used to love bread crusts.

My grandmother is a great lover of bubble and squeak. I asked her when she first remembers having it, and she said they'd had it since childhood. Another favourite was potato cakes.

Not much research or documentation exists to tell us specifically about our attitudes to food waste and how they've changed over time. And it doesn't appear to be something for which we have historically collected statistics.

We do know that the idea of avoiding food waste featured in cookery books published throughout the first half of the 20th century.

One of the most famous cookery writers at that time, who is still referred to by cookery writers today, was Mrs Beeton. She was born in 1836 and with her 'Book of Household Management,' which first came out in 1861, was the Jamie Oliver of her day.

Mrs Beeton died in 1865, but her books were reprinted and read throughout the early part of the 20th century and are still being referred to today.

An advocate of 'frugality', Mrs Beeton wrote that *The liquor in which a joint of meat has been boiled should never be thrown away.*[5] Mrs Beeton never had the pleasure of boiling (or 'braising') a joint of gammon in flat Coca Cola, but whatever the liquid used, it is always full of flavour and goodness and, as Mrs Beeton said, it should be put to good use as sauce, gravy or turned into soup or risotto.

We also know that food waste was a concern during World Wars I and II. There is lots of evidence of this in the posters and leaflets from the war years encouraging people to take care to make the most of their food.

5 Evans, D. et al. (2013) Waste Matters: New Perspectives on Food and Society, Wiley & Blackwell p. 12

Image: Pennsylvania poster, c. 1917. Special Collections, National Agricultural Library. [6]

Because some foods were in short supply during the war years, people needed to make the most of what they had. By 1915, sugar was rationed and by 1917, there were shortages of butter, margarine and meat and these became rationed too.

During World War II, rationing was introduced almost straight away, with eggs, milk, meat, cheese, sugar, butter/margarine and cooking fat, sweets and chocolate all restricted. Rationing continued until 1954.

During the war, it became a criminal offence to give pigs and chickens food that could be used to feed people. This meant they had to be given food waste. 'Pig bins' were therefore created, for people to put their food waste in.[7] These were still seen on London streets as late as 1953.

6 blogs.smithsonianmag.com/food/2010/05/american-food-posters- from-world-war-i-and-ii/#ixzz2iIMZEZtg

7 Edd Colbert speaking at Feeding the 9 Billion, Talk at The Royal Geographic Society for 21st Century Challenges series, 30th Octobter 2013. www.21stcenturychallenges. org/challenges/food-matters/media-gallery/video/edd- colbert/

Food writer and blogger Karen Burns-Booth spent a week finding out what it was like living on rations. The thing that surprised me the most was that she switched her plates to some that used to belong to her grandmother as they were smaller. The recipes she was using yielded much smaller portions than we have become used to.[8]

During the 1950s and 1960s advances in agricultural techniques meant that food production increased, food prices dropped and people became less concerned about wasting food.

Factory farming

Factory farming started in the 1930s in the USA, when it became common to raise chickens in cages, for both meat and egg laying. Chickens raised for meat were known as 'broilers' and those kept for eggs were known as 'layers'.

Prior to this, farmers would raise a few chickens, feeding them kitchen scraps and allowing them to roam around the farm 'grubbing' – finding bits of food to eat by scratching and pecking at the ground.

At the same time, the population was growing and becoming increasingly urbanised. More people living in cities meant fewer people keeping their own chickens. Some farmers realised they could benefit from this by producing more chickens and more eggs, to feed this growing population. They started to keep larger numbers of chickens, often in an indoor environment, so that they were all in one place and easier to manage.

Large numbers of birds mean lots of manure and lots of manure surrounded by lots of birds is difficult to

8 Karen Burns-Booth's blog post about war time rationing www. lavenderandlovage. com/2012/11/the-wartime-kitchen-living-of-rations-with-ration-book-cooking-day-one.html

remove. The broilers were only in their cages for a short time, usually around six weeks before they were sent for slaughter.[9] The cages were then cleaned out before the new batch of chicks was received.

Hens kept for eggs, the layers, presented a problem because they were kept for longer. When the manure wasn't removed, it increased the amount of disease. The chickens were dying.

Farmers started to use cages with slatted wooden floors or wire mesh so that the manure could drop through. This meant that manure could be removed without disturbing the birds and without interrupting their egg laying. The first cages were designed for individual birds or pairs. Then they started making cages for larger numbers of birds. Economies were also made by automating the watering, lighting and feeding. Saving labour meant saving money, and that meant cheaper food.

But what of the hens? Their natural behaviours are foraging for food, nesting, roosting and dust-bathing. When hens are kept in small cages they can't do all the things that are a normal part of chicken life.[10] This doesn't make for happy hens.

Part of the solution came in the form of injections of sulphur drugs to counter the contagious diseases, and vitamin D to compensate for loss of sunshine.

Problems also arose due to the stress the animals were suffering under these new conditions. Hens started injuring and cannibalising one another in their crowded

9 Compassion in World Farming (nd) Meat Chickens www.ciwf.org.uk/farm_ animals/ poultry/meat_chickens/
10 Compassion in World Farming (nd) Egg laying hens, www.ciwf.org.uk/farm_ animals/poultry/egg_laying_hens/

sheds.[11] To combat the fighting amongst the chickens they would be de-beaked to prevent injury. De-beaking involved cutting off part of the beak, often a third of the upper and lower beaks.[12]

Battery hens were very productive though, generally producing around 300 eggs a year in their first year of laying. Chickens live naturally for around six years. So, when their productivity started to decline, most commercial chickens were sent for slaughter, to make room for more productive birds.[13]

In the UK, factory farming started to take off during the 1960s. In 1946, 98% of UK eggs were free range. By 1966, only 8% of eggs were free range and by 1980 free range eggs accounted for only 1% of UK egg production.[14]

Images: Left: Battery Cage © Compassion in World Farming.

Right: Free range hens © Mayfield Eggs

11 Factory Farming and Animal Rights (nd) www.animalethics.org.uk/factory-farming. html
12 Factory Farming and Animal Rights ibid
13 Compassion in World Farming ibid
14 Adapted from data of MAFF and in the Museum of the British Poultry Industry, presented by www.fawc.org.uk/reports/layhens/lhgre007.htm, www.rspca.org.uk/ allaboutanimals/farm/pigs/keyissues

Factory farming then spread to pigs and cows. Instead of keeping pigs and cows outdoors they were raised in barns and stalls, which restricted their movement.

Sow stalls cause severe welfare problems, as the sow is unable to turn around, take more than one or two steps forward or backward, and most have no access to bedding throughout most of their pregnancy.[15] Sow stalls were banned in 1999 in the UK and since January 2013 have been banned throughout Europe.

What were the advantages of factory farming for people? It produced higher yields per acre of land and man hour of labour, leading to cheaper and more abundant supplies of food. However, this has come at a great cost to animal welfare standards.

New farm machinery

A significant effect on farming in the second half of the 20th century was the development of motorised machinery.

The first combine harvesters in Britain date from the late 1920s, but their use became more widespread after World War II.[16] An article in *Farming UK* states:

'Virtually no other invention has had the kind of impact on world food production that [the combine harvester] has had.' [17]

This machine performs three functions that used to require a great deal of physical effort from farm workers. The combine harvester cuts the crop, extracts the valuable grain with minimal losses and collects the grain into a large grain tank.

---

15 www.rspca.org.uk/allaboutanimals/farm/pigs/keyissues
16 www.reading.ac.uk/Instits/im/interface/advanced/farming/machines/machines_combine_harvesters.html
17 www.farminguk.com/news/75-years-of-combine-harvesters-in-Europe_19927.htm

Image: John Deere

By the 1930s, family and friends with pitchforks were starting to be replaced by the first mechanised balers. Whereas it used to be all hands on deck to get the hay in while the weather was fine, it is now done in a fraction of the time by far fewer people.

Therefore, arable farms also benefitted from an increase in productivity, bringing down the price of cereal crops and increasing the yields per acre.

Larger farms

With the mechanisation of farming, it was possible to farm larger areas with the same manpower. In the latter half of the 20th century there was a steady increase in the average size of farms alongside a steady decrease in the total number of farms. In 1951, the average farm size was 82 acres in the UK. In 1973, the UK joined the EU, giving farmers access to farm subsidies from the EU's Common Agricultural Policy. This almost certainly had a significant impact on the size and number of UK farms from 1973 onwards, and by 1975, the average size had increased to 126 acres.[18] In 2013, the average farm size was 218 acres.

When using farm machinery such as tractors, mechanised ploughs and combine harvesters it became apparent that larger fields took less time to produce the same yield. This was because it is quicker to use machinery in long straight lines rather than having to do lots of turns. This meant that having larger fields and larger farms made sense as it enabled farmers to increase their production still further, which in turn also helped to bring down food prices.

One of the side effects of this was that, in creating bigger fields, many hedgerows and field borders were removed. This was a problem for the wildlife that lived in the hedges and field borders, with many struggling for survival. Now when we look back on how farms have grown and how farming has intensified, we can see the problems this has caused for biodiversity. However, the consequences of what was happening have only recently become clear.

Observation and study have shown significant loss of species of flora and fauna due to man-made changes in habitat – changes like the removal of hedgerows. If seeds can't germinate and animals can't find breeding sites then numbers decline. A decline in one species can cause a series of problems for other species that rely on them. The RSPB's State of Nature report shows that 56% of UK species have declined since 1970.[19]

One such example is the decline in bee populations, which could have devastating consequences because we

18 Grigg, D. www.bahs.org.uk/AGHR/ARTICLES/35n2a6.pdf p183
19 RSPB State of Nature 2016, www.rspb.org.uk/community/ourwork/b/biodiversity/archive/2016/09/14/state-of-nature-2016-summary-of-the-report.aspx

rely on them to pollinate our food crops. One third of the food we eat is pollinated by bees and they also pollinate the flowers of many plants which become part of feed for farm animals.[20]

Agronomy – agricultural research

Between 1945 and 1970, new varieties of crops such as wheat, rice and maize were developed, and together with increased use of pesticides and oil-based fertilisers, and increased mechanisation this lead to far greater crop yields. This period is sometimes referred to as 'the green revolution'.

The age of abundance and invisibility of food waste

For several decades, food in the developed world became something of abundance. Throughout the 1980s and 1990s there was talk of butter mountains and milk lakes, which was due to the EU's Common Agricultural Policy food production subsidies leading to over-production. Flour and grain were cheap and plentiful and it is perhaps understandable that people became less concerned about food waste than their parents had been. With the new seemingly successful farming methods, people took this abundance for granted and assumed that food would forever more be cheap and plentiful. Consequently, food waste became invisible.

---

20 The British Beekeepers Association, Importance of Bees: www.bbka.org.uk/kids/ importance_of_bees

Quality standards

When I was growing up, my sister and I used to hunt for carrots that looked like a pair of trousers or potatoes that had a face.

If the apple I picked out of the fruit bowl had a brown bit, I'd bite into that first to see if it tasted nice or not. If it tasted bad I'd just bite off that bit and dispose of it, then eat the rest. The blemishes didn't bother me. That's just what apples were like.

It was only many years later that I realised that fruit and vegetables seemed to have become more and more perfect. What was the reason for this? Why could I no longer find 'carrot trousers'?

It was largely down to various quality and safety standards. There are rules about the bendiness of bananas and the curvature of cucumbers.[21] It became illegal to sell carrots that were forked or had secondary roots.[22] No wonder I hadn't seen 'carrot trousers' in years.

Image: James Wildman

---

21 Commission Regulation (EC) No 2257/94 of 16 September 1994 states that bananas must be 'free from malformation or abnormal curvature of the fingers'. Commission Regulation (EEC) No 1677/88 of 15 June 1988 states that cucumbers of Extra Class and Class 1 must 'be well shaped and practically straight (maximum height of the arc: 10 mm per 10 cm of length of the cucumber)' and that 'slightly crooked cucumbers may have a maximum height of the arc of 20 mm per 10 cm of length of the cucumber. Crooked cucumbers may have a greater arc and must be packed separately.'

22 Commission Regulation (EC) No 730/1999 of 7 April 1999 laying down the marketing standard for carrots states that carrots must be 'not forked, free from secondary roots'.

These rules weren't just spoiling the fun and games. They also created a lot of waste, adding to the amount of produce rejected by retailers and resulting in an increase in farm waste.[23] Many of these standards were about what the food looked like rather than what it tasted like or whether it was safe to eat. Tristram Stuart writes in his book, *Waste: Uncovering the Global Food Scandal* that: *'One way or another, supermarket standards in the West force some farmers to lose up to a third of their harvest every year.'* [24]

In 1970 came the introduction of the 'Sell By' date, first initiated by Marks and Spencer. There followed several different dates aiming to help people work out when food was safe to eat and when it wasn't. The 'Sell By' date was soon joined by 'Display Until' dates, 'Use By' dates, and 'Best Before' dates. These have since been nicknamed 'Confuse By' dates by food waste researcher and activist Jonathan Bloom.[25] The only significant date is the 'Use By' date as this is the only one that gives guidance as to food safety. Many people throw food away unopened simply because it is past its 'Sell By' or 'Best Before' date.

Before these dates existed, people used various methods to test the safety of food, such as the sniff test to see if it smelled bad – usually a pretty effective guide.

A new century and a new awareness

As the 21st century arrived, so did an increased focus on waste in general. Food waste was becoming visible again, which can be attributed to various factors.

23 Gille, Z. (2013) From risk to waste: global food waste regimes, in Evans, D.(2013) ibid
24 Stuart, T. (2009) Waste: Uncovering the Global Food Scandal, Penguin, p.102
25 Bloom, J. (2011) American Wasteland: How America Throws Away Nearly Half of Its Food (and what we can do about it), Cambridge, MA: De Capo Press

Landfill tax

Landfill tax was introduced in 1996 in the form of a tax paid on all waste that is disposed of in a landfill site. The aim of the tax was to make landfill a more expensive and less attractive option for disposal, so that companies and councils were encouraged to consider other options for their waste, seeing landfill as a last resort.

There are now two rates charged for landfill. Inert or inactive waste is charged at a lower rate, which in 2016 was set at £2.65 per tonne. The cost for waste that includes food waste was £84.40 per tonne in 2016.[26]

European Union legislation changes

The 1999 Landfill Directive set down ambitious targets to reduce the amount of biodegradable waste going to landfill to 35% compared to a baseline of 1995 levels.[27]

The Government put pressure on local authorities to improve household recycling services for bottles, cans, paper and plastics, publishing the 'Waste Strategy 2000 for England and Wales' in May 2000, which introduced proposals for statutory recycling targets for local councils.

Some years later, food waste collections came along, prompted initially by WRAP's work in this area, and some trial food waste collections that WRAP funded between 2007 and 2009.[28]

26 HMRC (2016) Landfill Tax, www.gov.uk/green-taxes-and-reliefs/landfill tax

27 Some countries, including the UK, have been given a four-year extension to this. European Commission (2012), Biodegradable Waste, ec.europa.eu/ environment/ waste/compost/

28 www.wrap.org.uk/content/local-authority-separate-food-waste-collection- trials

Increasing food prices

In 2008, food prices began to rise. This was due to the global recession and the impact it had on all businesses, including food businesses. Since then politicians in various countries, including the UK, have implemented 'austerity measures' to cut back on public spending to reduce Government debt. Governments around the world have had to reduce the amount of money they borrow and therefore reduce the amount of money they spend. Sometimes public services are cut and sometimes taxes increase. For example, in January 2011 in the UK, VAT (Value Added Tax) was raised from 17.5% to 20%. Although VAT is not charged on everything, and is not charged on food, any tax rise makes people feel everything costs more, so they may cut back on any spending that isn't strictly necessary. Just like when food prices fell, food waste increased, this period of economic austerity has perhaps contributed to a reduction in food waste, but given that this reduction is not shown across all EU countries, similarly affected by global recession, further factors are likely encouraging the positive effect on the food buying habits of many people.

Campaigns, activists and social media

In 2000, the UK government set up WRAP to improve recycling levels and create a market for recycled materials. They have since branched out into four strategic areas, one of which is food waste reduction. Their Love Food Hate Waste campaign was launched in November 2007 to raise awareness about food waste, help people learn more about food storage and give information on how to use up leftovers.

Think.Eat.Save is a global United Nations campaign, run jointly between UNEP and FAO[29] working to encourage people to reduce their food waste.

In recent years, there has also been a rise in the number of campaigners writing about waste. Tristram Stuart's *Waste: Uncovering the Global Food Scandal* in 2009 and Jonathan Bloom's *American Wasteland: Why America Throws Away Nearly Half Its Food (and What We Can Do About It)* in 2011 both highlight the food waste problem.

In 2013 and 2016, Rachelle Strauss' Zero Waste Week focused on reducing food waste, offering tips for better storage of food, providing tempting recipes to help use up leftovers and lots of information about how to plan and shop more effectively to save money and to reduce waste.

Relaxation of some cosmetic standards for food

In 2009, some of the cosmetic standards required of fruit and vegetables were relaxed by the European Union. This meant that certain fruits and vegetables no longer needed to adhere to strict specific standards governing their look and shape. Produce still had to be 'intact and clean, practically free from any visible foreign matter' which in plain terms means they mustn't be rotten or have any pests or diseases. That surely meant 'carrot trousers' were back on the menu? But no, it seems not.

It takes a lot more than simply changing the law. We need campaigning to get us to rethink what our fruit and vegetables look like in order to taste good. Our minds can play tricks on us, and long before we have taken the first bite, we have often already decided whether something tastes good or not.

29 See www.wrap.org.uk/unep

Many people think that supermarkets are to blame for the huge amount of wasted fruit and vegetables. However, we need to remember that supermarkets do their best to sell what they think their customers want. If the supermarkets think that customers will only buy vegetables that conform to a specific size, colour and shape, then that's what they are going to aim to sell, regardless of what is written up as Food Standards in law.

If we are to reduce the waste that occurs because the supermarkets set strict rules about what they are prepared to buy, then we need to let them know that we will support them in rejecting less food before it reaches the supermarket shelves.

There have been various campaigns, such as Tristram Stuart's Feeding the 5000 and the Gleaning Network, Hubbub's Pumpkin Festival and Hugh Fearnley-Whittingstall's War on Waste highlighting the enormity of waste these stringent standards result in and persuading us that looks aren't everything. Maybe as a result of such campaigns, knobbly veg is now creeping back onto supermarket shelves.

There has been a positive step forward across the board in supermarkets to relax cosmetic standards. Supermarkets, gardeners, green grocers and chefs would agree that wonky veg taste just as good and we are absolutely right to welcome back 'carrot trousers' or 'smiling potatoes'.

Increased consumer awareness

Now that most people in the UK have Internet access, it has become much easier to research the origins and production methods of the foods we eat. We are used to being able to find out about where and how our food is produced and we have come to expect information about sustainability to be included on company websites. This often includes information about how waste or by-products are dealt with and how packaging is minimised. This is enabling consumers to be more informed and demanding.

These days it is common to see sustainability information on food labels in large letters. Eggs that are free range will advertise that fact in bold lettering. Look a bit harder at some of the packaging of eggs that don't have the words 'free range' on the front. How hard do you have to look to find the words 'caged birds'? Did you perhaps even have to open the lid to look inside?

Food producers know that people think more about these things today, which is why they use positive messages to entice us to buy, and hide the more unsavoury details in the hope we won't see them.

Image: Enriched Cage © Compassion in World Farming

Increased visibility of food waste

There has been lots of publicity in newspapers, magazines and on television and radio about how much food we throw away unopened.

To see Hugh Fearnley-Whittingstall on national television point out to someone with a supermarket trolley piled high that they will throw away a quarter of what they buy is shocking to many people, but that is what the research tells us we are doing. That food represents a carbon footprint of 23.6 million tonnes in the UK in just one year. That means that each household in the UK is generating nearly a tonne of their carbon footprint just from the food they waste.[30]

As a result of all this campaigning, we are now wasting less than we were a few years ago.

---

30 These are figures are approximated and calculated from the WRAP Household Food and Drink Waste in the United Kingdom Report www.wrap.org.uk/ sites/files/wrap/ hhfdw-2012-summary.pdf

Case study – Waste2Taste

Waste2Taste is a business with a social mission.

Our vision is to set up Oxford's first permanent food surplus Café providing healthy, nutritious and affordable food with an ethical and sustainable approach, to address food waste, food poverty and homelessness.

The café will use food surplus as its main ingredients, and have a 'never waste anything' approach, creating a place for anyone and everyone.

The Oxford food bank are supporting our venture and we hope to gain the support of other suppliers and partners who share our ethos and vision. The café will provide mentoring and training opportunities to the homeless and vulnerably housed.

We have started on the path to attaining this vision by setting up an external catering service to build up our reputation and spread the word. Alongside this, look out for us at food markets, street fayres and Pop-up Bistro evenings.

We will be fundraising for the Gatehouse, Oxford.

You can follow our journey on social media:
facebook.com/waste2taste.co.uk
twitter.com/waste2tasteox

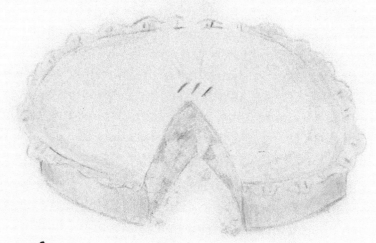

Why do we waste so much of our food?

Let's start off by looking at some of the reasons people give for wasting food.

Aesthetics

Sometimes we waste food because we don't like the look of it. Think of speckled brown bananas, bruised apples, floppy carrots, or brown lettuce. We think because it doesn't look its best then it is no longer edible. But that's not always the case. As discussed in the previous chapter, many of us seem to have an expectation that our food has to look perfect for it to be edible. We are used to seeing uniform fruit and vegetables, and plenty of choice too.

A regular discussion in the mornings as my children were getting ready for school involved the relative merits of each bit of fruit in the fruit bowl. This apple had brown bits round the stalk – rejected. That one had a bruise – rejected.

The National Trust, a key supporter of the Knobbly Veg Campaign says:

> *"Have you ever stopped to think about how perfect the fruit and vegetables in the shops look? Buffed to perfection, as if they're part of a village produce show.*
>
> *No wonder then, that so many British shoppers now see knobbly, dirty, scuffed produce as second best. But we should remember that they really do taste just the same!"* [31]

Fruit and vegetables have to be classified according to certain standards. The criteria don't just relate to freshness and certainly don't measure taste, but have a

---

31 The National Trust (nd) We Love Knobbly Veg (no longer available online)

lot to do with the way the product looks and they are given a class based on this. Shops must display the class of their produce and over the years they have wanted to offer only produce that meets the Class 1 standard. The produce that doesn't meet these criteria can still be sold, but the Class 2 label suggests that it is in some way sub standard. As the economy became wealthier and food comparatively cheaper, the Class 2 produce became less visible. Producers had to meet the demands of perfection and had to either find other ways to sell their Class 2 produce, such as by selling it to the food processing industry, or let it go to waste.

Over the last years, particularly with fewer of us growing our own fruit and vegetables, we've seen less and less of the Class 2 fruit and vegetables on display. We expect our fruit and vegetables to look a particular shape, size, or colour, so when it doesn't conform then we might expect it not to taste as good.

In 2009, some of the aesthetic standards were relaxed[32] and there has been lots of publicity and activity around encouraging people to change their habits and understand more about the relationship between looks and taste in their fruit and vegetables.

We have started to see more irregular shapes and sizes of produce in the shops and some of it is available at a lower price to encourage people to buy it.

Why not take a look next time you are in a supermarket and see what varieties of shape, size and colour you can find? Do all the fruit and veg look worthy of a photo in a picture book or is there more variety?

---

32 ec.europa.eu/agriculture/fruit-and-vegetables/marketing-standards/index_ en.htm. See also news.bbc.co.uk/1/hi/magazine/7724347.stm for an explanation of the changes

Some of the supermarkets are even creating slogans, to sell the benefits of this type of produce, and more recently they are actually marketing 'wonky vegetables' as a means of improving their green credentials.

Image: Anna Pitt

Habit

When preparing our food, we seem to discard much of it that could be eaten.

We peel the potatoes and throw away the peelings, when lots of the goodness is in the skin. We chop off the end of the cucumber and discard it. We chop off and discard the roots of leeks, the green leaves of spring onions and the stalks off mushrooms. We trim the fat off the meat. We use only the juice of lemons and limes. For what reason?

Is it just habit? Have we picked up wasteful habits from our parents and grandparents?

What was it my grandmother said about being fed up of having to scrimp and save? During the early part of the last century, people had to get every last ounce of goodness out of their food or perhaps had to go without. But with food becoming plentiful and significantly cheaper, people became less concerned about being wasteful. What mattered then wasn't getting the most goodness out of the food available, but having a plentiful supply of it. And so people got into the habit of only using the best bits of their food and buying and cooking more of it.

And the bits people discarded mostly ended up in the dustbin, which in turn went to landfill. No-one thought about the growing population and the proliferation of waste. No-one studied the effects of what happened to our food waste once it was in a landfill site. No-one had heard of the problem of global warming, or the dangers of leachate.

Because we didn't have to worry about the price of our cabbage, and we didn't realise that we were doing anything wrong, we got into the habit of pulling off the outer leaves of our cabbages and cauliflowers and tossing them into the bin.

However, we are now faced with the knowledge that before long we may have nine billion people to feed. We can't do that by being as wasteful. It's likely we will need some serious scientific research to look into the way we produce and process our food and our diets. For starters, it wouldn't hurt to think about using more of the food that we grow and buy. Cutting out some of our more wasteful and unnecessary habits will help.

Besides, have you ever tasted chopped, steamed and buttered cauliflower leaves? Have you ever snacked on the stalks from your broccoli? They are delicious.

Issues with portion size

Often, we waste food when we are served by someone else. No-one else can know how hungry we are, so how can it make sense for someone else to decide how much we would like to eat?

Most people don't consider food salvageable for another meal once it has been on someone's plate – whether or not the food has been touched. So maybe this is one of the key things we should try to fix.

Regulating our portion sizes so that we can finish everything on our plate, means being careful about how much food to take. When I serve myself, I can easily judge how much I can eat and I will then dip in for more if I'm still hungry (or even just because I like what I'm eating and can fit in a bit more without feeling too full).

How much I serve myself will depend on various factors, including how hungry I am, how much exercise I've had, how much there is to go around, when I last ate and when I'm next likely to eat. When considering how much to serve yourself you might also consider how much you like the food, as it will affect how much you eat if you are not keen on something.

Of course, portion size is also about how much to buy and cook as well as how much to put on our plates. For example, on many packets and in recipes you will find information about portion sizes, but I often find these don't work for my family and friends. So if you use a recipe or the instructions from the side of the packet and consistently find it is too much, then adjust the quantities. As long as you keep the proportions consistent, the recipe should turn out fine.

Working out how much to cook can be done quite scientifically. Love Food Hate Waste has a portion planning tool on their website,[33] which is perfect to get you on the right track whether you've just started cooking for yourself or your family, or you have decided to try to help reduce the food waste in your household.

Here's an example of some of the adult portion sizes they suggest:

- **Rice: 75g (I find this generous)**
- **Pasta: 100g**
- **Meat or fish: 140g (again I find this generous)**
- **Lentils, chickpeas or beans: 80g**
- **Fruit and veg: 80g for each portion of your 5-a-day**

Here are my top tips for making sure you cook and serve the right amount:

- Make sure you know the correct recommended portion for the most common foods, such as rice and pasta.

- If you don't have your scales in a handy place, then work out how much you need and then find a suitable cup that will give you exactly the right amount each time.

- Know who is going to be eating and when, so you know how many you are cooking for.

- Pre-plan what you can do with anything that you have left (e.g. lunch the next day, as an ingredient for the next meal, freeze for another time).

- Encourage people to serve themselves as they are the only ones who really know how hungry they are. Teach children as soon as you can to serve themselves.

33 Love Food Hate Waste Portion Planner www.lovefoodhatewaste.com/ portions/ everyday

- If you have never tried something before, take just enough to taste it first.
- Adopt the attitude that if it is on your plate you will eat it (unless you really can't). That way you will train your brain to only take what you need in the first place.

Lack of Planning

The main reason for wasting food is because we buy too much. What happens is that some of the food we buy goes off or goes out of date before we use it.

But why would we buy too much food? Isn't that just like taking some money out of our purse and stuffing it down the nearest drain? Well, yes, but of course we don't do it deliberately. We didn't mean to let that £2.00 coin drop out of our pocket and roll into the gutter, before we had even realised we had lost it. We didn't mean to throw away a quarter of the food that we bought last time we went shopping. Yet that's what many of us do.

We are most likely to buy too much food when we don't know what we need or how many people we are cooking for. When this happens, we might buy things that we like the look of, or are on offer, or that we usually buy. But how do we know how much to buy? Have we remembered what we have already in the fridge, the freezer and the cupboards?

Buying too much food often comes from lack of planning. Planning can take various forms and any amount of planning will help us make the most of our food and reduce the amount of food we waste.

In its simplest form, planning what food you need to buy involves being able to answer the following questions:

1. What meals will we want to have? Assuming most of us have three meals a day, which of those meals will be eaten at home or taken away from home?

2. How many people will be present for each of those meals?

3. Are there any special dietary requirements to take into consideration?

4. Can any of the required meals be provided from what is in stock at home already?

When I find myself shopping without a plan, I try to limit my purchases to what I know I need. If that's just one or two things, then that's all I buy. If I can't remember whether I have something available for the required meals before I'm next able to shop, I will buy something that could make a meal (or two or three) or could be put in the freezer or cupboard for future use.

Some people plan each meal meticulously and make a shopping list from that meal plan. Making the meal plan in the first place can be a fun thing to do, but I know from doing it myself, the planning itself can be hard.

Here are some tips to make meal planning easier:

1. Don't think you have to come up with something new and different for every meal. Old favourites can feature regularly on the meal planner.

2. Share the planning and ask each member of the family for their meal suggestion for one or two meals a week.

3. Consider a permanent three-weekly meal plan.

4. Think about two store cupboard meals each week in case of last minute invitations. If I use the store cupboard

ingredients, then I put them on the shopping list, if not, then I shift the store cupboard meal to next week's plan.

5. A friend has a blackboard in the kitchen where she has a weekly meal plan written up. She changes it when she thinks of something new to add or when she sees a dish she'd like to try.

Image: Jilly Jobling

Why not have a go at one of these ways of meal planning? See what difference it makes to your weekly food budget. You might be pleasantly surprised.

Too much information?

These days, lots of our food comes packaged with a mine of information printed on the labels. But do we read the information?

Do we check the ingredients before we buy to make sure that there is nothing in the product that we can't eat? Even the most experienced cook can be caught out occasionally with recipe changes or by forgetting to read the label.

The less processing involved in our food the less we need to read. A fresh banana in its skin, just as it has come off the tree, contains just banana. A processed version of the fruit, for instance dried banana might contain other ingredients such as sunflower oil or coconut oil.

The key bits of information that we want to know are often in small typeface, making them hard to read. Some information is fairly well hidden so as not to put us off our purchase.

Misconceptions/misunderstandings

I did a survey with a group of Year 8 students to see how many of us eat the fat off a piece of meat. Out of around 70, only 15 of us eat the fat. We talked about the reasons for not eating the fat. Someone suggested that the fat didn't look very nice. But most of the students believed that eating fat makes people fat. This is a common misconception. Eating too much food for the amount of energy you need is what makes you fat.

Fat is one of the five food groups and, as most of us probably already understand, we need to select foods from all five food groups as part of a balanced diet.

The fat on a cut of meat is a healthy part of our diet as long as we are moderating the amount of fatty foods we eat as a whole. The fat can add lots of flavour to our food.

It has become fashionable to choose extra lean minced beef for example but when browning the meat, people may then add additional oil to stop the meat from sticking to the pan. My preferred method would be to choose minced beef that retains a little of the fat from the cut of meat and not to add extra oil. This gives great flavour as well as less waste.

There are so many misconceptions about what parts of foods we can and can't eat. The next chapter along with the recipes in this book will explain how we can use more of what we buy.

'Use By' and 'Confuse By' dates

As covered in the first chapter, there are a range of dates on the food we buy, including the 'Sell By' date, the 'Best Before' date and the 'Use By' date. The only one of these dates that you, as a consumer of food, need to pay attention to is the 'Use By' date. The 'Sell By' date is for the shop staff to help with stock control and is being phased out by many retailers because it is known to cause confusion. The 'Best Before' date is supposed to give guidance as to the typical shelf life of a product and the 'Use By' date is a safety standard date for high risk foods such as meat, fish and dairy produce.

It should be noted, though, that all dates are estimated, based on typical and worst case scenarios. It is not true that if a food is within its 'Use By' date it is always going to be ok to use, and if it is outside its 'Use By' date it is never ok to use. A 'Use By' date is not going to protect us from poor food hygiene. You can't leave a joint of meat in the boot of your car for eight hours in 90-degree heat and expect it to still be edible just because it is within the 'Use By' date. Likewise, that strawberry yoghurt is unlikely to kill you because it's 'Use By' date says yesterday. The only solution is for us to get back in touch with what good, safe food looks like and smells like, and to make the decisions for ourselves. If it looks right, smells right and tastes right, then it probably is right. If it looks wrong, smells wrong or tastes wrong, then don't eat it.

My own rule is to think about the shelf life of a product in conjunction with the 'Use By' date as to whether I will eat something the day after this date. If something has a shelf life of a few days then I wouldn't use it beyond the 'Use By' date, but if it has a long shelf life before its 'Use By' date then I will consider eating it the day after the 'Use By' date. Having said that, the Food Standards Agency says this:

> *"'Use by' dates appear on foods that go off quickly. It can be dangerous to eat food past this date, even though it might look and smell fine. But if cooked or frozen its life can be extended beyond the 'use by' date."*[34]

Of course, the best thing to do is to check the dates regularly. You can then make sure you deal with everything on or before the 'Use By' date by either eating it, cooking it or freezing it. A 'Use By' date is technically considered to be up to midnight on that day.

If you are going to freeze something it is of course best to freeze it straight away after purchase, but you can freeze it any time up to and including the 'Use By' date to use it at a later date.

The length of time that food can be safely kept depends on the type of food, how it is prepared and how it is packed. A 'Use By' date is set by the manufacturer and is determined by various factors that affect the speed of microbial growth and the type of microorganisms that grow. This largely depends on the amount of water availability, the pH of the food (i.e. whether it is acid or alkaline) and the temperature at which it is being stored.

---

34 Food Standards Agency www.food.gov.uk/news-updates/campaigns/

Manufacturers use a range of predictive models and microbiological testing to determine the length of time a food can be safely kept.

There is no definitive list of which foods need a 'Use By' date and which foods don't. The types of foods that should have 'Use By' dates are as follows:

- Raw and cooked meats
- Fish
- Some pre-cut fruit and vegetables
- Some chilled ready meals
- Some sandwiches containing cooked meats, eggs or soft cheese.

There are really only two rules and they are:

1. Keep a close eye on any food that has a 'Use By' date and if you are not going to use it in time, cook it if raw (to eat within a few days) or freeze it.

2. Don't buy fresh food with a 'Use By' date if you don't know whether you need it. If you think you might need an extra meal, make it a store cupboard one then you don't waste it if you don't use it.

So, what about the other dates? Ignore them. If something is approaching its 'Best Before' date then it is sensible to use it up so that you are consuming it at its best. But if you've missed that date, then there are usually ways that you can use it up – and it is of course still safe to use – in a way that will improve its flavour, texture or appearance.

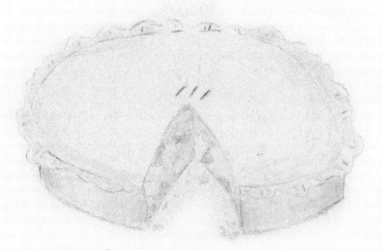

Making the most
of our food

How many people do you know who leave the crusts of their sandwiches?

I grew up with several cats and a dog, and we also kept geese, chickens, ducks and ponies all in quite a large garden. So, any food waste that came from our kitchen found a hungry mouth somewhere. So, whilst I've been separating my food waste from any other household waste for many years, and either feeding it to animals and birds, composting it or putting it into my wormery, not all that long ago I would readily be throwing away large quantities of food that we could have eaten because I was used to seeing it discarded, rather than served up on my plate. I had a narrow idea of what parts of our food can be eaten.

The ends of the cucumber, the leaves from a cauliflower, broccoli stalks and potato peel were regularly tossed into the 'goose bucket'. I thought it was normal and even necessary, to peel and discard outer layers of my food. It's what my parents and grandparents used to do.

Many of the offcuts that we throw away in the preparation of our meals can be eaten, and so much that we throw away is not just edible but also delicious and highly nutritious. All we need to make more of the food we have is a bit of know-how and imagination, plus a desire to make the most of every scrap.

Since learning more about food, food preparation and nutrition and taking an interest in reducing the amount of food I waste, I have changed many habits and made some interesting new ones. Now I try not to waste all the goodness in potato skins. The broccoli stalk is shared out as a pre-dinner snack; it also adds a nice crunch in a salad. Leek leaves and brown lettuce make great soup.

And there are many more ways to make more of what we have.

The nose to tail approach

The 'nose to tail' approach is a food philosophy that aims to use all parts of an animal. A similar approach can also be used with fruits and vegetables, sometimes known as 'root to fruit', whereby all parts of a crop that are edible in one form or another are used. Many top chefs have adopted this philosophy.

All food, whether it is from animals or from plants has a carbon and water footprint and a cost, not just a cost in financial terms, but in environmental terms too. It takes energy, time, water, physical resources and money to produce. These are all resources that should not be wasted. Out of respect for the environment as well as the people involved in producing food and the animals, if we choose to eat animal products, we should try to use up as much of it as we can.

Many of the recipes in this book will help you think about how to use up more parts of your food and to waste less of it.

'Nose to tail' or 'root to fruit' cooking is about more than just wasting less, though. It is also about enhancing the flavour and texture of our food.

Better food storage

Most of us could make significant savings in the amount of food we waste by understanding more about the rules of food storage.

Temperature guidelines for high risk foods

The danger zone for food is between 5°C and 63°C. This is the range at which bacteria can multiply efficiently. Foods that are being kept hot need to be kept at or above 63°C, and foods that are being kept cold need to be kept at or below 5°C to stop the growth of harmful bacteria.

Hot food should be eaten within two hours. After two hours, it needs to be stored in the fridge or freezer. You shouldn't place hot food straight into the fridge or freezer as this will cause the fridge/freezer temperature to rise, which could put other foods at risk and lead to condensation, which enables growth of bacteria. To ensure that food cools within the guideline time of two hours it is worth remembering that it will cool quicker if divided into smaller batches.

Cold food can be kept out for up to four hours. When serving any food, it is best to serve a small amount and then replenish it when the first serving is finished, to minimise the time it is left out.

Think about portion sizes when you put food into the fridge or freezer. Cooked food should be reheated only once, so if you are using up leftovers make sure you reheat the right amount. For this reason, it is useful to store the food in single portions, particularly when freezing. The freezer rule is this:

Food can be frozen **once from fresh and once from cooked**. If defrosting, make sure that you defrost food thoroughly before cooking. Some foods can be cooked straight from frozen.

What are high risk foods?

High risk foods are generally ready-to-eat foods like cooked meats and meat products, shell fish, dairy produce, cooked rice or pasta, foods containing raw or lightly cooked eggs and foods like sushi that are eaten raw. Foods are high risk if they support the growth of bacteria, i.e. they are high in protein and contain moisture. Although cooked rice and pasta are not high in protein, they are considered high risk because they contain high levels of moisture.

Raw meat and fish also need to be chilled until ready to cook. They are often not included in lists of high risk foods because bacteria will be destroyed by the cooking process.

When cooking and reheating it is important to note that the core temperature (that means the temperature right in the middle) reaches 75°C for a minimum of 30 seconds or 70°C for at least two minutes.[35]

Other food storage guidelines

Most fruit and vegetables can be stored in the salad drawer of your fridge. Pineapples, potatoes, sweet potatoes, onion and garlic should be kept out of the fridge, ideally in a cool, dark place. A cupboard in an unheated room is perfect. Bananas should also be kept out of the fridge and away from other fruit as they give off ethylene which causes other fruit to ripen. You can put bananas with any fruit that you would like to ripen a bit quicker.

---

35 Fellows, S. and Steadman P. 2015, Level 2 Food Safety Made Easy. Note also that in Scotland there is a legal requirement to heat food to at least 82°C when reheating. For more information about temperature control see Food Standards Agency, Maty 2016, Guidance on Temperature Control Legislation in the United Kingdom, www.food.gov.uk/sites/default/files/multimedia/pdfs/tempcontrolguiduk.pdf

In law this applies to food businesses, not householder, but it makes sense to follow these guidelines at home.

Dry goods such as flour, cereals, dried pulses, dried fruit and nuts should be stored in airtight containers. Storing such produce in glass storage jars looks nice and helps you to see what you have in stock. For long term storage, these goods also need to be protected from light. A cool dark place such as a cupboard or larder is ideal for long term storage.

Tinned food is a great way to reduce waste. Putting food into tins is a way of preserving the fresh food so that it lasts longer. The shelf life of canned foods tends to be anything between one and five years. Any date given is a guidance 'Best Before' date; so as long as the can remains undamaged it is normally fine to use after the 'Best Before' date. When you buy canned goods, make sure that you put your new cans to the back of your cupboard and bring the older cans forward. It is a good idea to go through your cupboards regularly and make sure that you take out any cans that are getting old and nearing or past their 'Best Before' date in order to use them. With all food, fresh, canned or frozen, remember the FIFO rule – first in first out.

Fridge management

Although your fridge is a tool to help keep food fresh it is still a short-term storage system and therefore needs good stock rotation habits to avoid unnecessary food waste.

When we think about food waste, we often think about the piles of rejected crops, spoiled harvest and surplus food at supermarkets and restaurants. We need to focus on the fact that 50% of food wasted in the UK is food wasted in the home.[36] The equivalent figure in the USA

---

36 www.wrap.org.uk/sites/files/wrap/hhfdw-2012-summary.pdf

is 43%.[37] Our fridges, or the way we use our fridges, are responsible for a lot of that waste.

For many fridges, the inside back wall is hidden by an army of jars or sauces, jams and pickles, obscuring everything that has had the misfortune to slip behind them.

A fridge does not stop the process of food decay, it just slows it down so that the food lasts longer. Many people will be all too familiar with the sight of a mushy cucumber, a bag of browning lettuce or a jar of pesto that has developed a fur coat.

Fridge temperature

Make sure that your fridge is at the right temperature. It should be between 0°C and 5°C and it is best to check this regularly with a thermometer. I usually keep my fridge at 4°C. My butcher recommends that if you have bought poultry, you should turn your fridge down to 2°C.

Fridge organisation

Rachelle Strauss, who runs Zero Waste Week,[38] suggests having an 'Eat me first' shelf in your fridge. This is especially useful in a house of several adults or for families with teenage children coming in hungry from school or from sporting activities, who regularly help themselves to something from the fridge to keep them going until the next mealtime. Rachelle's rule is that anything on the 'Eat me first' shelf is fair game for fridge foragers. Nothing on any other shelf can be touched. This avoids problems like new packets of cold meat or cheese being opened while the already open one languishes unnoticed behind the pickle jars. It helps if this shelf is the one

---

37 See refed.com
38 See www.zerowasteweek.co.uk/ for more information or to join

nearest to eye level as that it is naturally the first place foragers look.

The 'Eat me first' or 'use it up' shelf is the place to store leftovers, opened packets, unused portions of tinned food (in an airtight container not in the open can) and opened jars of foods such as pesto or salsa, that should be used up within three days of opening the jar.

Other than this, the rules of fridge organisation are that raw meat and fish should be stored below ready-to-eat foods, to minimise the danger of the juices from the raw foods contaminating foods that don't require cooking.

Fruit and vegetables are normally stored in a salad drawer at the bottom of the fridge. It might seem odd that these things are stored below the raw meat and fish, but they generally have a glass shelf above them so that juices can't leak through. If the glass shelf in your fridge gets broken, you should contact the manufacturer to get a replacement.

Stock rotation

For items that you have more than one of, it is best to have a clear rotation system. It is easy to have milk going off as you lose track of which pint was the most recent addition and which pint was the oldest. We no longer have this problem, since labelling the door shelves with a 'use from this end first' label.

Image: Anna Pitt

Seven tips to make fresh fruit and veg last longer
by Sally-Jayne Wright

• Cut celery across the stalks like this. If you separate the stalks from the root, your head of celery will not keep as long. The same tip applies to lettuce. Keep the root intact as long as possible.

• Take washed carrots out of the plastic and dry with kitchen roll or a clean tea towel.

• Keep Christmas clementines in the fridge not the fruit bowl. They don't like central heating.

• Eating half an avocado? Leave the stone in the other half and squeeze lemon juice over the flesh. Cover with the empty avo skin, wrap with cling film, then refrigerate.

• Remove strawberry leaves after washing, not before. Washed berries go mouldy and mushy fast.

• To keep spring onions perky, stand them roots down in a tumbler of water, like cut flowers.

• Wrap bunches of herbs in moistened kitchen paper, then wrap tightly in plastic bag, cling film or foil and refrigerate.

If you are not going to use something on or before its 'Use By' date, put it into the freezer to use at a later date. Remember, you can freeze something right up to midnight on the 'Use By' date. You can also extend the life of something by cooking it on the use by day and using it the next day or freezing as a cooked meal for use on a later date.

It is a good idea to have a weekly pot-luck lunch or dinner that uses up any vegetables, opened jars/tubs of sauce, leftover cooked meat or fish. Great recipes for this include soups, curries and risotto.

Once or twice a year, have a complete clear out of your fridge and put everything that needs using up onto the 'eat me first shelf' e.g. open jars of chutney, pickles, jam etc. Then set yourself the challenge of creating or finding recipes that make use of these ingredients. The 'Use-it-up' challenge can be great fun as a family event or for a group of friends.

Here's a recap of top tips for fridge management:

- Make sure your fridge is between 0°C and 5°C
- Always use the FIFO rule – first in first out
- Have an 'Eat me first' shelf for things nearing 'Use By' date or anything that's been opened
- Freeze anything you haven't used when it reaches its 'Use By' date
- Have regular sessions of using up everything.

Food banks and food sharing

Food banks are charitable or community organisations that collect donated food and distribute it to people unable to feed themselves or their families due to financial hardship. Most collect dry goods and tinned produce, as this makes storage easier to manage. They are generally run by volunteers and food is donated by members of the public or by supermarkets and other local businesses. Food banks will often have a shopping list of items that they need to be able to provide a balanced diet to the people who use them, so it is a good idea to contact them to find out what you can donate if you wish to help out.

People can need food banks for a number of reasons. These mostly involve a change in personal circumstances leading to financial hardship. This can include losing a job, bereavement or ill health. People are usually referred to a food bank by a doctor or care worker. The Trussell Trust[39] is a good source of further information about food banks in the UK. They currently run 424 around the country.

Food sharing

Food banks are a specific way of food sharing to help people in need. There are other ways of food sharing too that anyone can join in with.

There are several organisations who redistribute food and prevent it from going to waste. These include FareShare, Company Shop, OzHarvest, City Harvest, Feedback and the Gleaning Network. These organisations collect excess food from food retail outlets, food production companies, farms, markets, hotels, restaurants and catering companies and deliver it to organisations that can then make use of the food. They might deliver to lunch clubs, schools, community centres, food banks and community shops. They generally provide the food free of charge which means the organisations themselves

39 www.trusselltrust.org/what-we-do/how-foodbanks-work/

can save money on the food they have to buy in order to concentrate more of their budget on the services they offer, such as health, education and social care.

Some food banks or community food pantries do collect and redistribute fresh food. The food redistribution organisations listed can give further information.

These organisations usually take in food that is unsold at its 'Use By' date and find ways to turn that food into meals for future use. Some food surplus organisations can freeze perishable goods after the close of business on the 'Use By' date. This enables the goods to be used at future events. Many food retail businesses don't have the necessary facilities to freeze produce they don't sell and don't have the ability to turn it into a cooked dish in order to extend its useful life. So, there is a need for these businesses to partner with food surplus organisations that can do this for them. Disposing of food waste costs the businesses money. It is more cost effective to give it away to an organisation that can make use of it, rather than paying to dispose of it as waste.

Pop-up cafés or food surplus restaurants are a popular way of dealing with food surplus from local businesses and these often deal with fresh foods that would otherwise be unsold or uneaten. Pop-up cafés, restaurants and soup kitchens are often staffed by volunteers and they usually provide the food to their customers on a 'pay-as-you-feel' basis. This means people pay what they think the food is worth compared to what they might pay elsewhere, within the limits of their own budget.

Having attended several food-surplus events, I can strongly recommend them. Every event I have attended has produced delicious meals even though they have often not known the full list of ingredients they would be cooking with until they arrive to cook it on the day. They are also great ways to bring communities together, and to provide good meals for people who may not otherwise have freshly cooked hot food very often or who may not have the opportunity to enjoy the social side of eating food round a table together.

Food sharing apps

Another way of tackling the food waste problem is through the growing number of food sharing apps. There are apps like Too Good To Go which helps restaurants, cafés and other food businesses reduce waste by enabling them to offer surplus dishes to local people who are prepared to pick them up towards the end of their opening hours, at a greatly reduced price. Too Good To Go operates in several countries around the world.

For food at home, you can download an app such as OLIO, which allows people to share food they are not going to use with people in their neighbourhood. You can add your food to the list of foods on offer and it will alert people in the neighbourhood who are signed up to the app to let them know there is something available. Forty percent of items added to the app are requested within an hour. The team at OLIO says that 215,000 items have been shared in the 18 months since the app was launched and items have been shared in 41 countries. You can share all sorts, including food items that have been opened, that you don't like. It is a great way to clear out things that get left behind at a party. I have had bottles of ginger beer, lemonade, pots of cream, and packets of Skips, none of which my family drink or eat. Whatever it is you have, there will be someone near you on OLIO who does like it.

Gleaning and abundance groups

We are hearing more and more about how much fruit and vegetables are wasted without ever getting to a shop. There are several factors that cause fruit and vegetables to be discarded or to remain unharvested and left to rot.

We have already discussed the cosmetic standards of vegetables in the first chapter. Some crops are rejected by the buyers (e.g. the supermarkets) because they are considered not the right size, shape or colour to attract the customer to buy them. The buyers build in conditions to their contracts with the growers so that they only buy crops that meet their specified standards. As the way crops grow is affected by the weather, there are cases where whole fields of produce are rejected because they are too small, or the wrong shape or colour to meet those specified standards. If the contracted buyer doesn't want the goods, it is often not economical for the growers to harvest the produce to sell elsewhere when they don't have a guaranteed sale. This is because the harvest itself costs money.

The Gleaning Network was set up to combat this waste. It coordinates volunteers to harvest the unsold crop and passes the produce on to charities like FareShare and Foodcycle who then redistribute the food to people who need it.

In the last five years, The Gleaning Network has organised over 150 gleaning days and harvested 288 tonnes of food that would otherwise have been wasted. You can sign up to be a volunteer gleaner on their website. It is a fun thing to do and a great way to meet people while you are helping to reduce food waste and tackle hunger.

Abundance groups

Abundance groups tend to be smaller local groups of people who will harvest fruit from parks and gardens and common land and then make something from that fruit, like jam or juice. This can be sold at fêtes and the money raised put towards local projects. Abundance groups are often run through a Facebook page or group. You can offer your time to pick fruit, to make something with that fruit or if you have fruit trees or bushes that you don't make use of yourself, you can let your local Abundance group harvest it.

What we really can't eat and why

In the wealthier parts of the world, food is fairly abundant and relatively cheap. I think because of this we have become quite wasteful in the way we prepare our food. We peel a lot of fruit and vegetables and discard much of the skin, bones, organs and fat from meat, even though it is mostly edible, tasty and nutritious.

Having researched and written this book, I look back and realise that my family has wasted a lot of food that could have been eaten. I used to cut off and discard about an inch of both ends of a cucumber, just because I had seen my mum and my grandmother do it. I asked my grandmother why she did it and she didn't know. She said she thought her mum told her it was bitter at the ends, but she also said she hadn't ever tried eating them. I now use everything except the bit very close to the stalk and I haven't noticed any bitterness. I think it is a presentation issue; the ends are narrower so they don't give a nice even appearance.

When I wrote my first book, I had no idea that you could eat banana peel. It doesn't taste very nice raw, but when cooked it makes a good savoury snack (page 184) or ingredient for curry.

These days when we prepare food, my family tries to use the 'root to fruit' and the 'nose to tail' approach. If we want to peel our vegetables then we will use the peel to make vegetable crisps, or vegetable stock. We often cook meat on the bone as there's loads of flavour and goodness within the bones, and if we don't cook the meat on the bone, or if we haven't chewed and sucked the juices out of the bones (like lamb chop bones), then we cook them up to make stock (page 170) for use in risotto, soups and sauces. There are some mushrooms and fungi[40] we can't eat and there are plenty of poisonous plants and vegetables, and even some plants that we eat have poisonous parts. There are also certain mould spores that are very bad for us.

Things that we can't bite into might not be poisonous but because we can't break them down into pieces we can swallow and digest, we don't eat them, either because we could choke on them or because they could block our digestive system. Other mammals and fish have different digestive systems that are designed to swallow large things whole, such as bones and fur. This then stays in the digestive system for a long time while it is broken down. Humans are not designed for that.

So what can't we eat? The obvious answer is that unless it is poisonous then we can eat it. If you don't know that something is edible, then don't eat it. However, you may learn a few delicious new dishes made from things that you didn't know you can eat when you browse through the recipes in this book.

---

40 Wild Food UK gives a good guide to this: www.wildfooduk.com/mushroom-guides/

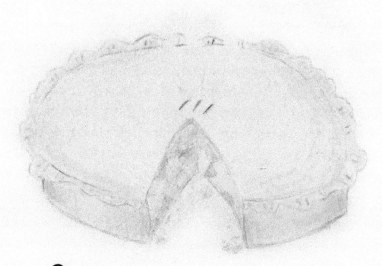

Growing your own

One way to avoid the rotting mass of shop-bought food is to grow your own so you can harvest what you need when you need it. There are lots of foods you can grow that will happily keep on growing for long periods allowing you to pick them as required.

You can grow your own food even without a garden. A plant pot on a sunny windowsill is enough for a mini herb garden. People often say they don't have time to grow their own food, but there are many things that once you have planted them, only need picking, though you may want to give them a bit of a chop back every now and then depending on how much space you have.

For no-nonsense no-fuss growing, you can't do better than devoting a bit of garden space to some herbs. All you need is to find a space, prepare the soil by removing the weeds and cutting back some other plants and then pop in your herbs. After that they look after themselves. Then just pick them when you are ready to use some in your cooking.

The following herbs are hardy perennials which means they come back every year.

Chives

Chives are easy to grow. They will grow pretty much anywhere and come back year after year with no looking after. You can even grow them in a pot on the windowsill. Chives have dark green grass-like leaves. In spring, they produce pretty pink mini football like flowers. They grow to between 20cm and 40cm in height. The leaves will disappear in the winter, but don't worry, they will be back again in early spring.

You can start off chives from a small clump from a friend's garden; remember to ask them first. Their chives will soon fill the space left by the clump you take and your chives will soon spread to wherever they can find room. Mine grow in the cracks in the paving slabs around my vegetable garden.

To harvest your chives, snip a bit off the top as and when you want to use it and you can happily cut them back to within an inch of the bottom and they will recover to produce more fresh leaf growth. Chives lend a nice peppery flavour to egg mayonnaise, green salads and soups.

You can eat the flowers too. Sprinkle them onto your salads or float them on top of your soups for a quirky decoration. Take a look at Wendy Shillam's roof top veg plot salad on page 145 for more edible flowers.

Fennel

Fennel quickly grows into a large plant with feathery fronds. It likes a sunny position. You can use various parts of the fennel plant including the bulb, but for that, of course, you need to grow several plants. Fennel has a liquorice flavour.

You can pick the leaves as you need them, to use as a flavouring for fish, as a salad herb or to make herb tea. If you like Liquorice Allsorts you may like to harvest a tub of leaves as a healthy alternative to the sweets.

The stems can be used like celery in salads or in cooking. Just pick the stems as and when you need them.

If you have lots of fennel plants then you can harvest the bulbs, which are delicious roasted or braised and are a common vegetable in Mediterranean cooking.

The seeds are a common spice in Indian and Middle Eastern Cookery. Harvest the seeds in autumn, by collecting the seed heads into a bag and then hanging them upside down for a couple of weeks to dry (with the bag wrapped around them to catch any seeds that fall out). Once dry, bash the bag against a hard surface such as the kitchen worktop to release the seeds from the seed heads. Keep the seeds in an airtight container for use in cooking or to sow next year. After a few days in a closed airtight container, open the container outside and let any insects escape. They will all have come out of the seeds to find oxygen. You can easily spot them and scoop them out. The seeds will keep their flavour for at least two to three years.

Fennel contains vitamins A and C and is a good source of Potassium and Calcium. It is known as a good remedy for indigestion, colic, and wind. It is also known to help rid the body of toxins, which can build up as cellulite.

Lemon balm

Lemon balm is a member of the mint family and the leaves do look similar to mint leaves but, as suggested by the name, they have a strong lemon smell. It is easy to grow and again, you can get started by pulling up a bit of a friend's plant, once you have checked with them that this is ok, making sure to pull out a bit of root with it. You can also collect seeds by cutting some of the flowering stems just as they start to turn brown; hang them upside down in a paper bag and wait for the tiny seeds to drop into the bottom of the bag.

Like mint, it is invasive, so you may want to contain it in a pot if you have a small space. It will spread via the roots so you will need to be ruthless with pulling it up if it isn't contained and is getting into places it shouldn't. You might want to cut the flower stalks off before they turn brown too, otherwise your lemon balm will propagate through its seeds too. It is easy to keep in shape by trimming it back and with its attractive leaf, lemon scent and pretty white flowers it is a nice plant to fill a gap in your garden, as well as being good for suppressing other weeds.

You can use your lemon balm for a relaxing tea and it is a tasty addition to salads. Lemon balm is said to aid digestion, ease headaches and it has antibacterial as well as antiviral properties. It has a mild sedative effect, so a drink for relaxation rather than invigoration.

Bees love lemon balm, so it is an excellent plant to have around your garden, simply for this reason. In order to attract bees, make sure you let the flowers grow, but the plants will give the best flavour when the flower stems are trimmed back. A good solution might be to grow one bush for culinary use, keeping it trimmed back to encourage compact growth and full flavor, and grow a second bush to attract bees to your garden.

Lovage

Lovage looks, smells and tastes like celery and can be used as a celery substitute. Its flavour is very strong so use it sparingly. It is easy to grow and to start you off you can divide a large clump by separating a bit of the root.

You can use lovage leaves in place of celery leaves or parsley. I use it mainly chopped in salads, and as a flavouring and garnish for soups. The young stems can be used like celery stems to make a good soup base, or steamed as a vegetable. The advantage of lovage over celery is that lovage is perennial, which means it comes back every year, whereas celery is biennial, meaning it comes back every other year. Lovage will die back completely in late autumn but don't worry, new growth will appear in spring.

Mint

Mint is a great herb for savoury and sweet dishes, and for drinks. Chopped mint is a popular accompaniment for roast lamb or lamb chops. I love adding some chopped mint leaves to fresh strawberries. A few mint leaves in some hot water makes a refreshing tea.

If you have a small garden you might like to grow your mint in a pot as it spreads from the roots and can take over a small garden.

Mint is easy to transplant and because it spreads easily your friends will probably happily let you pull up a bit of their mint, roots and all, to plant in your own garden or in a pot. It should recover quickly and will soon be taking over and spreading in your garden too.

Rosemary

Rosemary is a pretty evergreen shrub with needle like leaves, which is easy to grow in a sunny spot in your garden. You only need to keep it trimmed by eating it, as it can grow into a very large plant. In spring and summer, it has an abundance of flowers, which can be white, blue, purple or pink, depending on the variety. Rosemary is another bee friendly plant.

It is easy to grow from a cutting. If you take a 10cm cutting from a friend's plant you can put it into a plant pot, water it sparingly every few days and it will soon grow and be big enough to plant outdoors.

Rosemary is known as an accompaniment for lamb, pork and chicken, but there are lots of ways to use rosemary in your cooking and it makes a great addition to bread, stuffing and olive oil. Rosemary is said to help improve memory.

Sage

Bees love sage too and so do I. It is another easy to grow herb that is very hardy, will put up with most conditions and can thrive on neglect. It has velvety evergreen grey-green leaves and shoots up pretty pink or purple flower stems in late spring, so it is an attractive plant for your garden or window box. It is easily grown from cuttings, but takes a while to establish. It is therefore best left to grow for a year before you harvest the leaves. To harvest you simply pick a few stems and then pick the leaves from the stem to use them in your cooking. You can use the leaves whole or chopped.

Sage is a popular ingredient in the kitchen, particularly for flavouring pork, chicken, turkey and duck as it helps to break down fat. Sage butter is a tasty addition to pasta and gnocchi too, and it goes particularly well with pumpkin and butternut squash. Sage and onion stuffing is a favourite in our family and it is very easy to make. See the recipe on page 176.

Sage is said to stimulate the metabolism.

Thyme

Thyme is another pretty plant that looks lovely in any garden or window box. It has small grey-green leaves and purple, pink or white flowers. There are many varieties, the most popular being Common Thyme and Lemon Thyme. They like a sunny position, they are hardy and need very little looking after, but like most herbs they will benefit from frequent use, i.e. chopping back, which will encourage a compact growth.

They can be easily grown either from a cutting or by dividing the root of a large plant.

Thyme is a great flavouring for all kinds of foods and is one of my favourites for chicken. You can harvest your thyme all year round although growth will be more profuse through spring and summer. It can also be easily dried and stored. To use your thyme, you can either add whole sprigs that you will then remove before serving or you can hold the stalk at the top and use a thumb and finger to run down the stalk to strip the leaves and then you discard just the stalk, remembering to put it in the compost or food bin.

Thyme is a powerful antiseptic. It is a very useful cure for indigestion; a few sprigs of thyme in some hot water sipped slowly will help with the pain. It is also said to ease coughs as it contains flavonoids that relax the muscles involved in coughing, it reduces inflammation and loosens phlegm. In mediaeval times, it was thought to bring courage and ladies used to give their knights a sprig of thyme as they went off to battle.

This next group of herbs are annuals, i.e. they only last one year.

Basil

Basil is a great herb to grow in a window box or a pot on a sunny windowsill. Basil is not a hardy plant so you can grow it outdoors in a warm sheltered spot, better still, grow it in a pot as you can bring it inside when it starts to get cold.

You need to water basil plants little and often.

To harvest basil, pick leaves from the top rather than picking whole stems. It is good to harvest often as that will encourage growth. Remove any flowers as the leaves lose their flavour when the plant is supporting flowers. If you pick the flowers the flavour will improve in the leaves within a few days.

You can grow basil from seed or you can pick up a rooted basil plant and grow it on. To grow from seed, sprinkle the seed directly where you want it to grow and cover it lightly with a layer of compost. Make sure you wait until after the last frosts as even a light frost will kill young plants.

Basil is a popular ingredient in Mediterranean cooking.

Coriander

Coriander is best grown from seed, sown directly into the garden as it doesn't like to be transplanted. If you've ever tried to grow a coriander plant from the supermarket, you probably found it doesn't last too long. That's because coriander plants like to grow big and they have a long tap root that will grow deep down into the soil. If you do buy a coriander plant in a pot and want to grow it on your windowsill then you could try transplanting it into a deep pot to allow room for the root to grow.

Having said that, coriander is easy to grow from seed if you have the space. Scatter seeds around your garden or plant it in rows in your vegetable patch. The seeds will take around three weeks to germinate and you can harvest the leaves once the plant is around 10cm tall.

You can use the coriander leaves, the coriander seeds and even the root. When harvesting your coriander leaves, pick older leaves first to encourage new growth.

Coriander plants attract insects, which will munch on other less desirable insects that might attack your other vegetable crops so they are good plants to have around. You might not think that wasps and flies are good insects, but in addition to their natural pest control habit, they are important pollinators, so having plants that attract them is a good thing.

Parsley

Parsley is a biennial herb, although it will self-seed so you should get new growth year after year. There are two varieties: flat-leafed parsley and curly-leafed parsley. It is easy to grow indoors in a pot but it does like quite a lot of water so don't let it dry out.

It is easier to grow parsley from a plant bought at a garden centre rather than growing it from seed. If you do want to grow from seed sow indoors in a warm place in early March. They do take quite a while to germinate – up to six weeks – and you need to make sure you don't let them dry out completely during that time. The seedlings will be ready to transplant when they are about 8cm tall. Harden off your seedlings for around a week by putting them outside during the day and bringing them in at night.

When you harvest your parsley, it is best to pick the whole stem from round the outside of the plant rather than just the tips as picking the entire stem encourages new growth. Although, once established, parsley is hardy and will continue to grow over the winter; growth during this time will be slow and you won't be able to use much of it during the winter months.

Parsley is easy to dry and freeze, so it is a good idea to pick a bit extra in the spring and summer and leave it to dry thoroughly. Pick a bunch and tie a piece of string round the bunch then hang it up somewhere warm and dry. When it is completely dry, crush the parsley by hand. If it doesn't crush then it isn't properly dry so leave it a little longer. Store it in an airtight container such as an old jam jar, or freeze it in ice cube trays, so you can use a bit at a time.

Parsley is one of the most popular herbs in the UK. You will find it in lots of recipes. I like parsley sauce with vegetable bakes, steamed fish and with ham or gammon.

Parsley is a great way to get rid of garlic breath.

And finally, some vegetables

Courgettes

Courgettes are easy to grow from seed; you can keep a few seeds from courgettes that you buy. Plant them out in the garden or grow them in a container. Courgette plants, like all squashes, need plenty of room, so sow one or two seeds to a large pot or plant them a metre apart if you are planting them in the garden. Don't worry if you don't have a lot of space. You will probably get three or four courgettes a week from just one plant and regularly picking them will make them produce more.

Of course, if you forget to pick your courgettes, they will soon look more like marrows, especially after a bit of rain. I use bigger courgettes to make "courgetti" using a spiraliser.

You can use courgettes and marrows in many ways. If you have courgettes to spare, then you can make courgette cake. If you can't use all your courgettes, list them on OLIO (olioex.com) and you will soon find a neighbour who'd like a few.

Perpetual spinach

Perpetual spinach is actually neither perpetual nor spinach. Although it resembles spinach in look and taste it is in fact a type of chard. It can be used in all the ways you'd use spinach, but it is easier to grow. The more you pick the more it will grow and it needs very little maintenance.

You can sow perpetual spinach seeds in spring or autumn, in a seed tray and transplant the seedlings into your vegetable garden leaving about 6cm between each plant. Alternatively, you can sow the seeds directly into the garden. As the seedlings start to grow, thin the rows by picking out some of the baby spinach plants. You can then chop off the root and use the spinach leaves.

To harvest your spinach leaves, pick the leaves close to the base, taking a few leaves off each plant, unless you need to thin the plants in which case you can pull up an entire plant root to make space for the other plants to get bigger. As you pick the outer leaves the inner leaves will grow bigger and the plant will produce more leaves at the centre.

If the outer leaves start to wilt or go brown or get eaten by insects, pull them off and discard them onto your compost heap and the plant will be encouraged to put on new growth.

The easiest way to wash your spinach is to fill the sink or a bowl with enough water to completely cover the leaves. Let the leaves soak for a bit and then gently swish them about to release any grit or mud. If you are going to use your salad leaves raw, dry them off in a salad spinner.

Spinach is pretty hardy so your plants should keep on growing right through the winter. Just keep on picking and eating.

Pumpkins

Pumpkins are big plants so they will need a lot of space. They are easy to grow from seed and there are lots of ways you can cook with your pumpkin. Keep a few of the seeds next time you have a pumpkin, wash off any of the flesh and pat them dry with a tea-towel. Spread them out on a baking tray or container and store them somewhere cool and dry. When the seeds are dry, put them in an envelope or paper bag to store ready for planting the next spring. They will take about a month to dry completely, which is important as otherwise they may go mouldy.

Plant your seeds in April. Sew a single seed into a small pot filled with compost. Once the plants have germinated and they look sturdy enough to stand up to the weather, transplant them into a large pot or in the garden. I usually plant half a dozen seeds, but remember you need plenty of space for each plant so you could give away some of your small plants to your friends if they all germinate successfully.

As your pumpkins grow, it is best to raise them up off the soil so that they don't rot. You can prop them up on a piece of wood, or an old tile to keep them off the ground.

I harvest my pumpkins as I need throughout October and November. You don't need to worry about a few blemishes or a bit of insect damage on the skin, as this will not affect the taste. If you leave them on the plant throughout the autumn they will keep on growing. When the pumpkins are fully mature, the stems start to crack and the skin hardens. To test if your pumpkins are ready to eat, prod the skin and if it indents then it is not yet ready, so leave it a little longer. To pick your pumpkin, cut the stem leaving at least 10cm of stem on the pumpkin. If you don't leave a bit of stem, the pumpkin is more likely to rot. You need to harvest your pumpkins before the first frost. If you are not going to use your pumpkin straight away, give it a chance to harden a bit more by putting it in a frost free sunny location for a few days. You can then store them in a cool dry place for up to six months, so you can have a whole winter of pumpkin from just one or two plants.

Remember, remember the 5th of November but remember pumpkins are for eating, not just for carving out lanterns.

Tomatoes

My favourite crop to grow in the garden is tomatoes. I particularly like cherry tomatoes and they are very easy to grow. Traditionally, many people grow them in a grow bag, but thanks to a water saving tip sent in by Frank for my first book, *101 Ways to Live Cleaner and Greener for Free*, I've recently been planting mine directly in the soil. Grow bags are great if you only have a yard or very small garden but they do dry out quickly, so need lots of watering. The advantage of planting tomatoes directly in the soil is that this allows them to send out much deeper roots and enables them to look for their own water. That way they only need watering in prolonged dry spells.

Tomato plants can be grown easily from seed, sowing them indoors in February or March. The seedlings take a couple of weeks to germinate and then they will take another six weeks or so to get big enough to transplant into larger pots. Be careful not to overwater your seedlings, and keep them away from frost and cold draughts.

You can plant them outside in a patio pot, hanging basket, grow bag or directly into the ground once all risk of frost has passed.

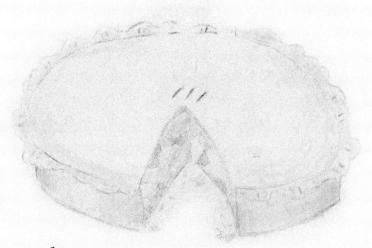

What should we do with our unavoidable food waste?

Despite all these ways that we've looked at to help us reduce food waste, there are some parts of our food that we just can't eat. No matter how much we plan and how thrifty we are, we will always produce a certain amount of food waste.

If we accept that food waste will always be produced, let's look at some of the ways we can deal with it, that can benefit us and be kinder to the planet.

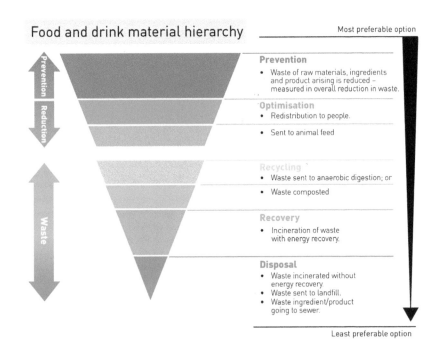

Image: WRAP

Animal feed – The Pig Idea

Historically, one of the main ways of dealing with food waste is to use it as pig food. Pigs are very efficient at turning food waste back into two useful resources: food i.e. pork meat; and manure to use as fertiliser.

Pigs like a varied diet and they are naturally omnivorous, just like we are. That means they eat meat as well as plants. However, they do have preferences. Ben and Jerry's, the ice cream makers, feed most of their food waste to pigs, but they found that the pigs don't like their mint-flavoured ice cream.

What happens when the food waste contains pork meat? We think that being cannibalistic, i.e. eating the meat of one's own species, is a dreadful thing, but pigs don't think that way. Pigs are naturally omnivorous and even cannibalistic. They don't mind a bit of pork with their lunch and will happily eat sausage and eventually turn it back into sausage – a perfect circular economy.

Despite being an efficient way of turning food waste back into food, feeding food waste to pigs has, in some parts of the world, become less commonplace. In the UK in 2001, for example, an outbreak of Foot-and-mouth disease that affected the whole nation was thought to have originated on a farm that was illegally feeding unprocessed food waste to its pigs. In response, the government banned the feeding of restaurant waste to pigs. The ban was originally intended to be a temporary measure, but it was later recommended that the ban be continued, and in 2002, the ban was extended across the whole of the European Union. At present, treatment of food waste is governed by the Animal By-Products Regulation, which is regulated by the Animal and Plant Health Agency.[41]

With feeding food waste to pigs banned, pigs are generally given grain crops such as soya, wheat and maize. However, much of this grain comes from previously forested parts of the world, such as the Amazonian rainforest, and clearing forest to grow grain crops is contributing to

---

41 www.gov.uk/government/organisations/animal-and-plant-health-agency

global warming in a big way. Furthermore, while we are not feeding our food waste to pigs, we are having to find other ways to deal with this waste. Over the past few decades we have been mainly putting food waste in our general waste bin, much of which goes to landfill sites, where it rots down and releases greenhouse gases and leachates which are further contributing to pollution and global warming.

Feeding pigs on cereal crops that farmers have to buy in also makes pig farming much more expensive. So that makes the meat more expensive. It is estimated that feeding grain to pigs instead of food waste more than doubles the price of raising a pig. The response to rising costs of raising pigs is two-fold. Some farmers have chosen to stop raising pigs in the UK and others have overcome the problem by raising more pigs in the same amount of space.

The figures show us that in the UK today, we are eating the same amount of pork as we did prior to the food waste ban, but we now have to import lots of our pork. In 1998, there were 8.1 million pigs in the UK. In June 2013, the UK pig population was just 4.8 million. Importing food generally means a higher carbon footprint, due to the transport emissions.

What about raising more pigs in the same space to make the same profit? We looked briefly at the problems of factory farming in chapter one. My belief is that all farmed animals must be kept in conditions that are best for their health and wellbeing and that, in turn, is what's best for our health and wellbeing.

The ban on feeding food waste to pigs has only ever, in fact, included certain types of food, like plate waste and cooked food from restaurants and school canteens. There has always been lots of food that remains legal and safe to feed to pigs. Examples of this are bread, hops that have been used in brewing, and unsold fruit and vegetables.

Often when legislation such as the food waste ban is brought in, a lot of confusion results and that's why lots of this allowable waste food is forgotten or missed as a possible food source for pigs, in favour of specifically grown grain based feeds.

How do we make outdoor reared pork more sustainable? That's what The Pig Idea is campaigning to do.

Firstly, the Pig Idea would like to see more pigs fed on the allowable food waste that's produced, and secondly, they are campaigning to have the ban removed so that other waste can be used as an additional food source.

The Pig Idea team have been raising their own pigs at Stepney City Farm in London. These pigs are fed a nutritious diet of local organically produced okara, the leftover parts of the soybean, which is a by-product of making tofu. They also eat whey and mixed vegetables from a local dairy, fruit from a local greengrocer and spent brewers' grains from a brewery (the grains after they've been used for making beer). All these foods, that would otherwise have been wasted, give the pigs a varied diet without competing for land for human food crops or requiring further deforestation.

In the future, the Pig Idea would like to see the EU ban on feeding catering waste to pigs overturned. They point out that it is possible to ensure the correct systems are in place so that the food waste is treated correctly.

The people at the Pig Idea suggest we should learn from countries like Japan and South Korea where surplus food is properly treated and turned into pigswill. The meat from pigs fed on such swill is considered a delicacy as the varied diet is said to improve the flavour.

In November 2013, The Pig Idea organised The Pig Feast, an event in Trafalgar Square in London when top chefs prepared and cooked some of the pigs that they had raised at Stepney City Farm, and offered a free lunch to 5,000 people.

Speaking to people at the Pig Feast event about their thoughts on feeding food waste to pigs, as well as what they thought of their free pork lunch, I was surprised how many people had no idea that pigs weren't fed on food waste. This highlights that many of us have really become detached from the process of how our food is grown or raised.

It is important that we understand the food chain and how what we eat and the way we get our food to the table impacts on our environment as well as our health. Here's a summary of how we can take action:

1. Be aware of where our food has come from and how it has been grown or raised.

2. Support local high welfare farming.

3. Support campaigns that are fighting for sustainable food and farming. If you don't like the idea of campaigning through adding your name to social media campaigns or joining events, you can campaign by being careful where you spend your money.

Anaerobic digestion

Another way to deal with food waste is to use it to create energy and fertiliser via a process called anaerobic digestion (AD). AD is a way to turn organic waste such as food waste, garden waste and animal manures into useful resources. The organic waste is known as the feedstock.

'Anaerobic' means without oxygen and the AD process uses the bacteria in the feedstock itself to break the material down. The food and other waste is chopped up in a machine like a big blender and made into a kind of feedstock soup. It is then fed into a 'digester' tank, which is sealed to keep the air out. It is like a big stomach, where good bacteria break down the food particles to release the nutrients.

Just like we have to feed our stomachs a balanced diet, the AD tanks need a balanced diet. But here's the difference... Our stomachs sometimes get a bit windy, particularly when we eat certain foods. Most of us don't like it when that happens. However, in the AD process we want this to happen. So, the scientists mix the sources of food and green waste and slurry into just the right proportions to maximise the emissions. It's those emissions, a combination of methane and carbon dioxide, that are captured as biogas.

Biogas is made up of around 60% methane and 40% carbon dioxide with tiny amounts of other gases, known as contaminants. The exact mix of gases depends on the particular mix of feedstocks. The idea is to maximise the production of methane, which is the combustible part of the biogas. Combustion of the biogas is used to produce electricity, heat, or both.

The biogas can be burnt directly to release energy, or it can be refined into pure methane and fed into conventional gas-fired power plants. This is referred to as bio-methane.

When the maximum amount of digestion has taken place and as much gas as possible has been captured, what remains is known as digestate. This is a useful source of natural fertiliser, as it is rich in nutrients, which farmers can use on their fields to improve the soil.

To really understand the importance and value of the digestate part of anaerobic digestion you need to know a little about fertilisers. All plants need a number of nutrients to grow. The main nutrients required for healthy crops are nitrogen, phosphorous and potassium. These are known sometimes as N, P and K (the atomic symbols of the nutrients, which are all elements). These three nutrients are known as the macro nutrients and are the main constituents of fertiliser. It is estimated that without fertilisers we could only feed half of the world's current population.

Let's look first at nitrogen. Nitrogen is important to plants because it is a constituent part of chlorophyll. Chlorophyll is what a plant uses for photosynthesis, the plant's method of making food for growth. Nitrogen, is abundant in gas form in the atmosphere, but is rare in solid form within the soil, and gets taken up by the plants themselves as they grow. It therefore needs to be replenished within the soil if the soil is to continue to support efficient plant growth.

One way to replenish the nitrogen in the soil is to grow a crop of legumes such as alfalfa, broad beans or clover. Such plants fix the nitrogen from the air into the soil, thanks to bacteria on their root system called rhizobia. The bacteria combine nitrogen molecules with hydrogen to form ammonia. This becomes stored in the plant as amino acids. As the leguminous plants die, all the nitrogen within the plant is released back into the soil as the plant rots down, forming a natural fertiliser.

For many years, farmers, particularly in the intensively farmed parts of the world, have used synthetic fertilisers to replenish nitrogen and other nutrients. Synthetic fertilisers were developed in the early part of the 20th century to increase food production yields to feed the growing population.

Just like the natural process that goes on in a field of legumes, the production of synthetic fertiliser also combines nitrogen from the air with hydrogen (usually methane gas) to form ammonia (NH_3, an alkali) using processes such as the Haber-Bosch process or the Birkeland-Eyde process. The ammonia is then usually combined with acid such as nitric acid to make it into a salt, which is then applied to the soil as fertiliser.

Making synthetic fertilisers is an energy intensive process as it requires high temperatures and high pressure. Furthermore, the hydrogen is derived from natural gas, which is a fossil fuel. This means that synthetic fertiliser is harmful to the environment it is designed to help.

Phosphorus is another vital nutrient for plant growth. Phosphorus fertiliser is made by extracting the phosphates from mined sedimentary rock. The phosphates contained within the rock are separated from other particles such as sand and clay. There are two methods of doing this, known as wet or dry processing. The dry method involves treating the rock phosphate with electricity. The wet method involves 'washing' the rock phosphate with an acid such as sulphuric acid to produce phosphoric acid.

While atmospheric nitrogen is effectively unlimited, the global reserves of phosphate rock are finite. It is estimated that current usage rates would lead to reserves of phosphate rock being used up within 50–100 years.[42] This means that we need to start thinking about ways of recovering phosphates from other sources to ensure that we don't exhaust supplies.

That's why anaerobic digestion is such a useful process, as the digestate is a way of saving phosphorous that would otherwise be lost if we just threw away our organic waste. Digestate produced as a result of AD can replace synthetic fertiliser and in doing so it saves energy and fossil fuels and therefore reduces carbon emissions.

As with any fertiliser, it is important to apply the digestate at the right time of year, so these nutrients are taken into the soil. If the digestate is over applied or applied to the soil in times of heavy rainfall the nutrients are likely to be washed off the land and end up in the watercourses, where it does more harm than good. This is known as 'eutrophication'. AD facilities therefore have storage areas for the digestate fertiliser so it can be sold to farmers at the time of year that they need it.

In the UK, many local councils (the organisations involved in collecting waste from households) have a separate container for food waste. The food waste from these collections is often taken to an AD plant, which means that your food waste is utilised in a useful way. You may be asked to use special compostable bags for your food waste, but in fact it has been found that

42 Houses of Parliament UK Post Note Number 477, August 2014
researchbriefings.files.parliament.uk/documents/POST-PN-477/POST-PN-477.pdf

these compostable bags don't break down anaerobically. Composting is an aerobic form of breakdown (i.e. with the aid of oxygen), so these bags have to be removed during the AD preparation process. Using compostable bags if your collection is going to AD is therefore no different to using plastic bags. If your food waste collection is being taken to a compost facility it is important not to use plastic bags because as the compost dries and the bags open up they can get caught in the wind and blow away. They then become a source of pollution. However, a number of AD sites are now accepting plastic bags for the collection of food waste as they are equipped to remove all plastic packaging at the start of their process.

Some local authorities mingle green waste and food waste together for treatment in a composting facility. When this is the case, the problem with non-compostable bags is that the material will not degrade through the composting process if it is not EN13432 compliant material (the European Norm for compostable packaging)[43] so will remain in the soil for many years.

Another alternative for lining your food waste bin is newspaper. The newspaper breaks down anaerobically, so this is better than using the compostable bags or plastic bags.

It is important to use the separate food waste container if you are provided with one. This is because it is much better from an environmental perspective as well as being cheaper to dispose of food waste by anaerobic digestion or composting than the alternatives of landfill or energy from waste (incineration). However, this only works out if people use the facility. If you look at the economics of the system you can see why. At the time of writing, where

---

43 www.compostme.co.uk/standards.html

I live, sending food to anaerobic digestion rather than energy from waste costs 2.5 times less. If a council offers a separate food waste collection, but only a quarter of the people use it, they have the same operating costs but only a quarter of the budget saving with which to cover those costs, because they are still having to pay 2.5 times more money for the waste of the other three quarters of households who don't bother to separate their waste.

There is a move by a number of local authorities to move to two-weekly, three weekly or even monthly residual waste collections which would give them significant savings. To do this, however, they need to collect the food waste weekly to prevent it smelling in the bins.

Composting

If you have seen a compost heap in action, you will know just what I mean when I say that composting is a form of alchemy, converting organic waste into "black gold", creating a virtuous circle of using food grown in soil to feed the soil again by composting food waste.

This has a scientific explanation, and it is all to do with decomposition; that decomposition takes place with the help of various organisms, microbes, moulds and bacteria, which feed off your waste and in doing so help to break it down.

A compost heap will produce carbon dioxide and heat as it breaks down. The heat helps the bacteria to work faster and that speeds up the decomposition process.

So where does the goodness in compost come from? The basic elements of the organic material that went on to the compost heap are not lost. All organic material is made up of carbon and a combination of six macronutrients:

nitrogen, phosphorous, potassium, sulphur, calcium and magnesium as well as a range of micronutrients such as iron and copper. These nutrients are all elements and when the organic material breaks down through the composting process these nutrients remain in the resulting compost where they become available for use by new plant growth. When the nutrients are available for use like this, they are described as bioavailable.

What you can compost

You can compost any biodegradable material. Composting meat and cooked food is generally not recommended because they can attract pests.

However, there is lots that you can compost and if you follow a few basic rules your compost will be a lovely sweet smelling resource for your garden.

Composts need to have a balance between nitrogen-rich feedstock and carbon-rich feedstock. This is sometimes referred to as a mix of 'greens' and 'browns' with the 'greens' being the nitrogen-rich materials and the 'browns' being the carbon-rich components.

Watch out though, because the green and brown labels can be a bit misleading. Many a nitrogen-rich substance is in fact brown; take for example tea leaves and coffee grounds. And don't think that you can only compost things that are green or brown.

The nitrogen-rich 'greens' include:
- kitchen waste such as fruit and vegetable peel
- grass cuttings
- weeds from the garden
- cut flowers or flowers heads from deadheading
- fresh leaves
- hedge clippings
- algae and pond weed.

The carbon-rich 'browns' include:
- nut shells and stones from soft fruit such as plums
- bread or rice
- wood ash
- dry leaves
- newspaper
- shredded paper
- the woody parts of shrubs
- toilet roll and kitchen roll tubes
- small quantities of cardboard
- eggshells
- chopped up twigs and small branches
- pencil shavings
- small pieces of fabric (from natural fibres)
- pine needles and pine cones
- sawdust
- cotton wool
- paper napkins and tissues.

At first I couldn't understand why dried leaves were a 'brown' and fresh leaves were a 'green' when essentially, they are the same thing. All organic matter contains both carbon and nitrogen and all organic matter has a carbon to nitrogen ratio. This is sometimes shown as the C:N ratio. How do we know how much carbon and how much nitrogen something contains? It is all to do with the amount of water content. Fresh vegetation has a higher water content than dried vegetation.

For the ideal compost conditions, you need around 25 parts nitrogen to 1 part carbon. That doesn't mean you need 25 times more 'brown' than 'green'. Both the 'browns' and the 'greens' contain a mix of carbon and nitrogen, it is just the proportion that varies. Most composting experts suggest that you use twice the quantity of brown compared to green, but as long as you introduce at least equal the amount of brown to green you should have an effective compost. If you have too much 'brown', then the compost heap won't be doing very much in terms of breaking down, as it is harder to generate the necessary heat when the carbon content is too high, as it mainly comes from the nitrogen; if you use too much 'green' there is a danger that nitrogen will be lost to the atmosphere.

In terms of value of the compost for your garden, you don't want to be losing an essential nutrient that is so hard to get back. In terms of your personal comfort, you don't want to lose that nitrogen, because it escapes in the form of ammonia, which smells of rotten eggs.

You can also put human and pet hair on your compost heap, although this takes a long time to compost as well as things like latex gloves and chewing gum, although these will take a good length of time to break down.

If you want to make the best possible compost for your garden it is helpful to catch weeds before they go to seed otherwise the seed will be in your compost and may well germinate when you apply your compost to your garden.

Bokashi

Bokashi is a form of composting that uses microorganisms to ferment food waste. In Japan, where the method originated, it was traditionally done by covering the food waste with a rich soil that contained the microorganisms naturally. It is in fact another form of anaerobic digestion.

Most people tend to think of bokashi composting as using a special bokashi bran to cover food waste in a lidded bucket. The advantage of using a bokashi bucket is that it is known as a good method for breaking down cooked foods, and particularly meats. Here's why:

• Bokashi is a closed system using a lidded bucket so no rodents or insects can get in.
• Bokashi systems break down food much faster than traditional composting methods.

The reason you need to use a lidded bucket is that bokashi is an anaerobic method of breaking down organic matter. It is more of a fermentation rather than a composting process. It is not actually the bran that's doing the breaking down. It is the microorganisms that do all the work. They are a special mix known as Effective Microorganisms or EM for short. The EM are sprayed on to the bran, which acts as a carrier, so that the EM can be stored, transported and applied to your food waste as needed.

The microorganisms consume the sugars from the organic waste, which causes the fermentation to take place. The fermentation process takes about two weeks after which time the organic waste is broken down sufficiently to add to your compost heap without the worry of it attracting flies and rodents, or you can dig it straight into the soil.

Because bokashi fermentation takes place at a low pH, very few greenhouse gases are produced. This is because the methane producing microbes typically found in anaerobic digestion tanks and in traditional compost heaps are unable to survive at a low pH level.

The main microbes in the bokashi bran include lactic acid bacteria (LAB), yeast and purple non-sulfur bacteria (PNSB). Each of the different types of bacteria has a specific job to do and the mixture of bacteria also means that they work together as a whole. As the microbes start to feed on the sugars in the food waste, they multiply and that speeds up the fermentation process. Some organisms also begin to feed on the waste of other organisms in the system. For example, the PNSB feed on any dead yeast and LAB bodies. The LAB will consume some of the waste of the PNSB. The LAB can break food down without producing gases.

Another advantage of using bokashi over traditional composting is that you don't need to worry about what quantities of 'green' and 'brown' waste you put in your bin.

Wormeries

Wormeries are similar to compost heaps, but with a little added help. The difference between a wormery and a compost bin is that you set it up to make it the best kind of environment for the worms to process the waste into soil. You do this by creating a habitat that the worms thrive in. Then of course, you add worms.

In the UK, we have 28 native species of worms. The most common type of worm in the UK is the Common Earthworm or Lumbicus terrestris. As you probably know, earthworms are very good for the soil. They burrow through the soil, making holes, and therefore allowing air and water to circulate through it. As they feed, worms help to break down organic matter, such as leaves and dead plants and animals. You may be familiar with the worm casts they leave behind at the end of their digestive process. These worm casts are full of nutrients from the broken down organic matter, but the important thing is they are now in a form that is available to living plants that are growing in the soil, rather than locked up in the dead parts of plants and animals on and within the soil.

There are certain species of worm that are so good at breaking down organic matter in the soil that they have become known as 'compost worms'. Compost worms native to the UK include Eisenia andrei, also known as red wrigglers, Eisenia fetida, also known as Tiger worms, brandlings or manure worms and Dendrobaena veneta, which are known as Dendras or European night crawlers.

Most suppliers of worms for wormeries provide a mixture of different composting worms and these worms will happily get along together. As different varieties of worm thrive in different conditions, having a mixture of worms will mean that your compost is looked after for you as the conditions change over time according to the weather and the type and amount of waste that you are feeding your wormery. As the worms themselves will be changing the soil conditions as they process the waste, the mix of different varieties of worm will mean that the worm population should remain balanced according to the waste to be treated.

What does a wormery look like and how does it work? It usually consists of a layered bin or bucket, with two or more layers. Each layer of the bin needs to have drainage holes that are also big enough for the worms to pass through as they work their way through from one layer to the next as they process the waste. The lid of the bucket will also need to have small holes so that air and water can pass through, but these holes must be small enough that other creatures can't get in.

Wormeries often have a collection area underneath for the liquid. This liquid is the rainwater and moisture from the waste with lots of dissolved minerals and particles. The liquid makes excellent fertiliser for the garden. Use it diluted with 10 parts water, on lawns, vegetable gardens, patio pots, flowerbeds or even for houseplants.

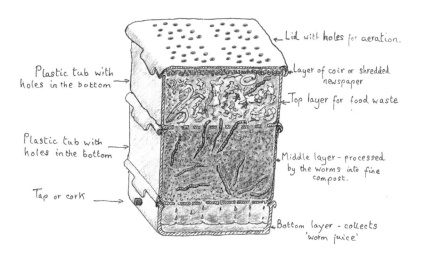

Image: Jo Lewington

When you first set up the layers of your wormery, add a small amount of old compost or soil to the bottom layer and then add your worms on top of that. They will start to burrow down into the compost as they like to be in the dark. Then add a layer of food waste over the top of the compost and worms. The worms will gradually start to process the food waste, turning it into a rich compost. As the worms process the food waste they will reproduce and you will have more worms able to process more food waste.

When the first layer is full, place the new layer on top and start to add your food waste to the new layer. When they finish processing the waste in the lower layer, they move up through the drainage holes into the upper layer to start processing the waste there. Once the worms have finished processing the waste it looks like rich, black soil and, used sparingly, is perfect for your garden. The process takes between three months to a year.

When all the wormery layers are full you need to empty the oldest tray, which should be the bottom tray. Take off the upper trays so you can remove the bottom tray. Place the upper trays back on the wormery and then place the bottom tray (the one you are going to empty) on top of the wormery, to check that it is ready. You should find that all the food waste is well rotted and it looks like the compost you get from the garden centre. You should also notice that there are hardly any worms in this layer. If you leave the layer on the top with the lid off for a short time during the day, most of the remaining worms are likely to burrow their way down to the layers below as they always move away from the light. Once the worms have gone you can empty most of the lovely rich compost out to use in pots or in the garden, leaving behind a handful to mix with your new kitchen waste. Don't worry if you lose a few worms along with the compost you are using. They will soon find some old leaves or other decaying vegetation somewhere in the garden outside the wormery.

Most composting worms don't like the soil to be too acidic. They prefer a pH of between 6.5 to 7.0. For this reason, you will often hear people mention that citrus fruit peel and onion skins are not good for wormeries. You can add these in moderation, but if you have a lot, it may be better to have an ordinary compost heap too. You need to make sure you balance these acidic foods with plenty of less acidic foods. If you have a lot of pot worms (enchytraeids), which are tiny white threadlike worms, this is an indication that your wormery has become a little too acidic. These pot worms are harmless and in fact will also be composting the waste for you, but they can manage a lower pH than the tiger worms. You can counteract the acidity of your wormery either by introducing a special lime mix that you can buy for wormeries or by adding some crushed eggshells.

It isn't the nice fresh kitchen waste that the worms will be eating. The food needs to have rotted down before the worms can digest it. That's why your worms might seem a little slow to process your waste. It is also the reason why you may occasionally find that your wormery starts to smell. If you are introducing too much fresh waste compared to the partially rotted waste the worms are working on, then it sometimes ends up putrefying. The solution is to hold back on the waste and let the worms catch up. You can get your rubber gloves on, find a trowel and push some of the newer food waste into the partially processed compost. Another useful trick is to add a bit of shredded paper or torn up cardboard, but avoid the glossy paper from magazines as the worms are not so keen on this. The paper or card helps to introduce air into the compost. Without air, the decaying process turns anaerobic and the worms can't live without oxygen, so they are not going to be assisting with the breaking down of the food in the parts of the wormery that have become anaerobic. If you mix in some air, and stop feeding new waste for a while, your wormery should recover and the worms will get back to work. Once the worms catch up, the smell will go away.

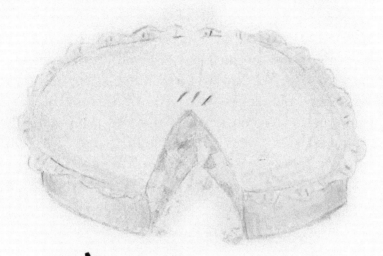

What if we just
throw it all in
the bin?

Well that depends on where you live and how your local council opts to deal with general waste.

Energy from Waste using incineration (burning)

Your general waste might be sent to an Energy from Waste plant. Energy from Waste (EfW) involves applying a thermal process, in the form of incineration, gasification or pyrolysis, to the waste to create heat or electricity or both from the combustion process. Incineration is at present the most usual form of thermal processing. The general waste is burnt at very high temperatures and there is a process to capture the resulting energy. Many people consider that dealing with waste this way is better than sending it to landfill.

Energy from Waste plants have four basic processes:

• A reception area to receive the waste and get it ready for combustion. This might involve removing some materials that can be recycled or removing hazardous items.

• The combustion process, which releases the energy from the waste.

• Conversion of the energy (heat and gases) to a transportable form, e.g. electricity or fuel.

• Emissions clean-up: making the waste gases safe and recovering metals for reuse.

Why is EfW considered better for the environment than landfill? Landfill produces carbon dioxide (CO_2) and methane (CH_4) in roughly equal proportions whereas energy from waste produces CO_2 only. Both these gases contribute to global warming, although methane is around 25 times more damaging than carbon dioxide.

Lots of the waste that we burn is plastic, which has to be burnt at temperatures in excess of 850°C. This is so that the gas output is not toxic. The problem with having large amounts of food waste in the feedstock is that it has a high water content, which naturally lowers the temperature as moisture is released on contact with heat. If you put a tray of roasting potatoes into a hot oven you can see the water vapour that is given off and your oven temperature will plummet. So, food waste is not an ideal feedstock for energy from waste by incineration, whereas it is an ideal feedstock for other forms of making energy from waste such as anaerobic digestion. But that can only happen where people separate food waste from their general waste and where the facilities exist for this separated food waste to be collected.

Landfill

Your council may still be sending general waste to landfill, in which case that's really bad news because food waste in a landfill site will rot away, create methane as it rots and the leachate that results can mix with other substances in the landfill and become toxic. Dealing with food waste in this way changes it from being a useful resource to an environmental hazard.

Leachate

As the microbes in our waste food break down, the texture of the food will change. It will either dry up, as the water content evaporates, like autumn leaves, or become squidgy, like rotting cucumber. As a cucumber rots, a greenish liquid comes out of it. Other organic matter is the same, but just may take longer than a cucumber, which is notoriously short lived once picked.

This liquid is leachate. Leachate in itself is not harmful. That green liquid oozing from your cucumber isn't going to do any harm on its own. It is when leachate mixes with other substances that it can become dangerous.

When the leachate in landfill mixes with rain water and then with other substances from mixed waste, particularly things like batteries, fluorescent lightbulbs, and metals, it can become corrosive and toxic; if leakage occurs then it can pollute watercourses and becomes harmful to the environment, as it de-oxygenates the water, killing fish, and reducing the number of invertebrates.

We are getting better at designing landfill sites and we line them so that in theory there is no leakage. Most landfill sites also ban hazardous substances and electrical items. This would be okay if everyone understood, kept to the rules and never put anything in their waste bin that was disallowed. However, it is most unlikely that no one ever makes a mistake and of course, it isn't feasible to check every bag of waste that ever gets to landfill.

Greenhouse gases

As organic matter breaks down it produces gas. The gas from landfill is generally about 40–60% methane, with the remainder being mostly carbon dioxide. You may have heard of these gases being talked of as greenhouse gases. Greenhouse gases contribute to global warming by acting like a coat trapping in the warmth from the earth's surface. When you put a coat on, you are not expecting it to warm you up, so much as to help you retain your own body heat. That's what greenhouse gases are doing. They are keeping the heat from the earth, which comes from absorbing the sun's energy, around the earth rather than letting it escape back out into space. We are quite good at regulating our body temperature by wearing the right clothes. When we get hot we wear fewer clothes so that we lose heat. There comes a point that we need to add a layer, so we put on a jacket. We add layers of clothes as we cool to stop our remaining body heat from escaping. But imagine if you weren't in control of your layers of clothing. Imagine you had spent an hour running on a warm summer's day and someone made you put on a jumper, and then another jumper and then a coat. That's what is happening to the planet as we layer up the greenhouse gases around it. This has a knock-on effect: the rise in overall temperature is resulting in a lower percentage of ice and snow coverage. With less snow and ice covering the earth's surface we have less surface area that is reflecting the sun's energy back up towards the sun. This is furthering the global warming process.

What if you don't have a separate food waste collection and don't have room to compost at home?

Some councils have introduced separate food waste collections and then found that they can't continue with them because people are not making use of the system. As explained in the previous chapter, this results in a situation where the council has the cost of the separate food waste collection without the savings from not having to send the waste to EfW or landfill.

Other councils don't have an economically viable place to send their food for composting or anaerobic digestion yet. If they do start to offer the service, you will be able to do your bit by making sure you separate your food waste to make the new scheme work.

Some people manage to find local organisations that are able to take their food waste. If people are consciously minimising their food waste by following the suggestions in this book, then it is possible to save it up and take it to a local allotment or farm, or to give it to a friend or neighbour who can compost it.

All avoidance of food waste in whatever form it takes is important and worthwhile. Whatever little bit you can do to avoid wasting food and to help others avoid waste is a step in the right direction.

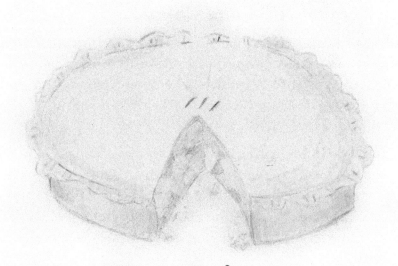

The future
of food

"If food waste was a country, it would be the third largest emitter of carbon dioxide equivalent gases behind only the USA and China." [44]

We need to change this. As well as needing to reduce carbon emissions to minimise global warming, we also need to take into account the growing population and how we are going to be able to produce enough food in a sustainable way.

There is no doubt that we need to make some changes to our food system so that it becomes sustainable. The great news is that there are many ways we can do this. There are already lots of people making small changes in the right direction and loving our leftovers is a big part of that.

Let's look at what a sustainable food system might look like.

More plant, less meat

Some parts of the world that have traditionally eaten a largely vegetarian or vegan diet are starting to eat more meat and dairy.

Meat has a higher carbon and water footprint than a plant-based diet. There is an increasing awareness that our dietary choices have an impact on the planet. Now that people are realising this, many are choosing to make more of their meals plant based. This doesn't mean we all need to become vegan. It just means that more of us need to be more selective about how much meat we eat.

---

44 Food and Agriculture Organization of the United Nations (nd), Food Wastage Footprint and Climate Change www.fao.org/nr/sustainability/food-loss-and-waste

Traditionally, most of us eat in the morning, around the middle of the day and again in the evening. That's 21 meals per week. Assuming many of the meat eaters have around a third of meals meat free without thinking about it, reducing the number of meat-free meals by another third should still be fairly easy. Perhaps we could then further reduce our reliance on meat so that we have two or three meat-free days each week. Part-Time Carnivore has developed a calculator that shows you how much land, carbon emissions, and water you save by choosing meat-free days. The carbon saving of having three meat-free days a week looks like this:

Image: Part-Time Carnivore

Why not see what your meat-free days save? You can try out the calculator at www.parttimecarnivore.org.

I feel that farm animals are an integral part of our landscape and I don't want that to change, but I do want to see an end to factory farming and intensive monocultures that harm our environment.

When I first started shopping and cooking for a family I thought that most people shopped once a week, so I did that too. I used to think I needed to buy seven lots of main meals, and to me at the time, that meant buying seven lots of meat or fish. I have since learnt that there are different ways to plan and shop to feed my family, ways that save me money, reduce waste and are less stressful and time consuming than a weekly shop. We now view meat and fish as a treat and have it mainly at weekends. The star of the show is a roast dinner on Sunday. This might then provide leftover meat for other meals during the week or to freeze for future home-made ready meals. I am essentially buying just two or three meals of meat for the week. This saves me a lot of time and money. Locally-reared meat fed on a locally-sourced feed is less carbon intensive than animals that have been transported long distances or fed on a diet that has been intensively farmed and transported for many miles. So, although I am still eating meat, by making it a treat and not an everyday essential, I am reducing my impact on the planet.

Localism and seasonal eating

We have come to expect that we can buy everything, anywhere and at any time of year. However, this results in many miles of transportation and an unnecessarily high carbon footprint. The most carbon intensive produce is anything that has been airfreighted. Food producers and retailers don't usually tell us if produce is airfreighted. I try to guess if I can't find the information, and I avoid buying something if I think it is airfreighted. If produce can be shipped there will be lower emissions, but do we really need to have apples and strawberries all year round? In the UK, for example, could we not just be content with apples from October to May and then enjoy strawberries instead in June and July and blackberries in August and September, in line with when they are available locally. For a sustainable future, we need to reduce the carbon emissions of our food system. To reduce emissions from food transportation we need to be aware of where our produce comes from and how it is produced.

Vertical/urban farming

It is thought that by 2050, 80% of the predicted nine billion global population will live in cities. To feed this nine billion people we will need more land to grow more food. However, we can't get more arable land without chopping down trees and we know that chopping down trees is bad for the planet. The carbon footprint of one hectare of deforestation is 500 tonnes of CO_2, which as Mike Berners-Lee expresses it, is *'equivalent to an average car driving 28 times round the world'*.[45] Instead it makes sense to create more space for food production by going up not out. Vertical farming is a way of growing more in less space and this gives the opportunity to bring food production nearer to the people who are going to buy and eat it. It is particularly suited to fast moving crops like lettuces, tomatoes and leafy greens.

Plants need water, light and nutrients to grow. Vertical farms use aquaponics or hydroponics, which involve drip feeding the plants with water that has nutrients dissolved in it. Aquaponics uses fish waste to provide the necessary nutrients and hydroponics uses digestate. Ashley Lydiate, of Blue-Sky Greenhouse, a vertical farm in London, explained to me that hydroponics uses 70% less water than conventional farming methods as well as being more carbon efficient by using fewer chemicals, and by lowering the transport emissions by growing food nearer to where people live. Vertical farming methods can

45 Berners-Lee, M (2010) How Bad are Bananas: the carbon footprint of everything, Profile Books

be used indoors and even underground making efficient use of space and nutrients from waste streams. Lydiate considers the factors that affect taste and explains that when produce is grown intensively it is given fertiliser that boosts the fruit size rather than giving it the micronutrients and time to develop flavour. Rushing the ripening process diminishes flavour, so we need to find efficiency in other ways. With further research Lydiate suggests that vertical farming with these kinds of soil-less technologies can produce a crop that is equivalent to an organic crop in terms of taste and flavour, and being chemical free. He feels that we need to encourage people not to be afraid of high tech food and to taste it for themselves. Another similar technology that can be used at home or in schools is vermiponics which uses 'worm juice'. You can use the liquid produced by a wormery to grow lettuces in a plastic bottle using a wick that draws up the liquid as the plants need it.

Insect protein

Growing in popularity is the idea that we can get some of our protein requirements from insects rather than from meat, fish and seafood, dairy or plant-based proteins such as soya and tofu. Insects are a good source of protein and are considered to be a strong possibility for sustainable diets as they require less feed than our traditional meat based proteins such as beef, lamb, pork, or chicken, and they produce less waste. Cows need to eat 8g of feed to gain 1g of weight whereas crickets need only 2g of feed for 1g of weight gain.[46]

The Food and Agriculture Organisation of the United

46 Dossey, A., 2013, Why insects should be in your diet, in The Scientist, February 2013 edition www.the-scientist.com/?articles.view/articleNo/34172/title/ Why-Insects-Should-Be-in-Your-Diet/

Nations has estimated that insects already form part of traditional diets for over two billion people.[47] But for those of us who are not used to the idea of eating insects there is a definite 'yuk' factor. However, people often don't like the idea of certain foods, without ever having tasted them. I have eaten mealworms and crickets and both were very tasty. I could definitely eat those in a salad as a substitute for bacon bits.

Closing the loop on waste

One of the most important things to reduce food waste, is that we become more efficient at using more of the food we produce.

Reading Tristram Stuart's book, *Waste: uncovering the global food scandal*, one thing that stuck in my mind was the sandwich maker who was required by their customer to discard four slices of bread from every loaf, the crusts and the next slice in from the crusts, which is around 17% of each loaf.[48] This is so that the sandwiches look good. We expect our shop bought sandwiches to be a certain shape and size. My immediate thought was to wonder why the sandwich maker didn't supply the bread to another supplier to make bread and butter pudding (see page 207).

The reason behind this waste was down to the aesthetic standards imposed by the powerful customer (i.e. the supermarket). If we examine the issue a bit further, though, the supermarket considered consumers in general thought that the look of the sandwich is of greater importance than the carbon and water footprint

47 van Huis, A. et al, 2013, Edible Insects: future prospects for food and feed security, Food and Agriculture Organisation of the United Nations, 2013 www.fao.org/docrep/018/i3253e/i3253e.pdf
48 Stuart, T. 2009, Waste: Uncovering the global food scandal ibid

to produce it (taking into account any wasted food). In addition, the supermarket perhaps considered that its customers either would not know or would not care about the wastage. In other words, waste was an acceptable part of the supermarket sandwich and was largely unseen and not thought about as something unethical.

Thankfully today, we are realising the extent of the food waste problem and many of us are starting to do something about it. The more we, as consumers, know and understand what waste is produced by whom and why, the more likely it is that our hugely wasteful society will change its ways and waste less.

Supermarkets are looking into ways to reduce waste and many small businesses are finding ways of turning otherwise wasted produce into foods.

Two of my contributors, Rubies in the Rubble and Snact are using fruit and vegetables that would otherwise be wasted. Rubies in the Rubble make jams, chutneys, pickles and ketchups, all from surplus produce. In their London Piccalilli, they use misshapen cucumbers that are rejected because they won't fit through the machine that supermarkets use to wrap their cucumbers. Snact makes fruit leather by dehydrating fruit. This fruit leather or fruit jerky, as it is also called, is just made with fruit. There is no added sugar or preservatives, so it is like eating a piece of fruit in terms of the nutrition but more transportable, and of course it is helping to solve the problem of food waste by using fruit that isn't otherwise going to be sold either because it is the wrong size, the wrong shape or colour for the contract it is being produced for. Snact originally started making their fruit leather from surplus fruit that was unsold at the end of the day in London's wholesale markets. Now they work directly with farms and this year plan to save 50 tonnes of food from going to waste.

These are just two examples of the growing number of companies successfully managing to address the food waste problem in innovative ways. Making our food go further is a good way to reduce the impact of food production on the planet and to ensure that we have enough food for our entire population without resorting to more intensive farming, further deforestation, soil degradation and pollution, all things we now know are harmful to the environment. Even food waste we think is unavoidable can be turned into a saleable product. Bio-bean is another company tackling the problem of food waste using spent coffee grounds from our huge coffee culture to produce renewable energy in the form of coffee fuel. Bio-bean's factory can process 50,000 tonnes of coffee grounds a year. There's still plenty of room for expansion though, as this represents only one in 10 cups of coffee drunk in the UK. Bio-bean are researching other uses for coffee grounds to further replace fossil fuels with this renewable fuel.

I am pleased and also greatly relieved that food waste is now a hot topic. I get very excited hearing Monica Galetti praising Masterchef contestants for using up all the edible parts of the plant or animal. I was delighted to be part of the Sainsbury's Waste Less Save More launch talking about my family's experience of Zero Waste Week and discussing ways that supermarkets can help themselves and their customers to waste less food. We talked about people having seen speckly bananas being thrown away at the end of the day and we wondered why Sainsbury's didn't turn them into banana bread. Now, they do. There is always a way to close the loop and to cut down on waste. We just need to find that way. Wherever there is waste there is a way to turn that waste into something delicious, we just need to be more creative or look back in history and see what less wasteful generations or populations did or do to make better use of the bits (see pages 163 to 176). There are so many possibilities and opportunities and young people are driving forward a food revolution that will change our wasteful ways.

This was never more evident than at Dan Barber's wastEd pop-up restaurant in Selfridges, London, during Spring 2017.[49] wastEd's menu was a feast of dishes created from by-products and off-cuts. Afternoon Tea featured delights such as 'charcuterie scrap quiche with blueing cheddar', 'cod head brandade with vegetable ash mayonnaise and potato skins' and 'buttermilk scones with mango peel marmalade'.

While I was at wasteEd, I met a couple from the USA who run a café and we were chatting about what they did to reduce food waste. They told me they offer their spent coffee grounds to customers for use in their gardens. Coffee is not only a great fuel, but also an excellent addition to compost. Then they told me that they were concerned with the plate waste produced, so they went to talk to a local pig farmer and now they save their plate waste for the farmer to turn into feed for his pigs, showing that this practice is still acceptable in the USA.

To me, such examples show that if people are aware and care about reducing avoidable food waste and making better use of the unavoidable food waste then we can ensure a sustainable food system for the future.

During my research for this book, particularly for this

49 www.selfridges.com/GB/en/content/article/wasted-london

last chapter, I have seen and read about many examples of different food systems and new technologies, but sometimes I think we just need to look behind us. For too many people food has just become a commodity stacked high on supermarket shelves, always there, always replaceable, and divorced from how and where it was grown or reared. I think the future of food is about reconnecting with how, when, where, by whom and with what resources our food is produced. My hope for the future of food is that we will buy less of it, but reap more from it. Food grown and prepared with love and respect is always going to taste better. Will that be your future of food?

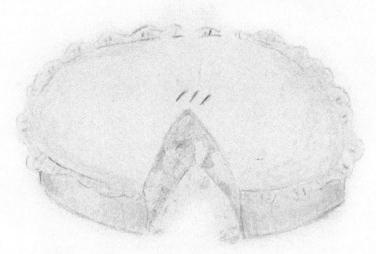

Making the most of your meat

Chicken and Leek Pie

If I roast a chicken on a Sunday, I generally have enough meat left to make at least two more dishes for the week. We love to have this one mid-week and it is the original Pitt family Leftover Pie.

Makes 1 x 25cm pie

For the filling
- 2 leeks
- a knob of butter
- leftover cooked chicken (if short on chicken, feel free to swap in some bacon or ham)
- 1 tin of sweetcorn, drained
- 500ml white sauce (see page 197)

For the pastry
- 150g plain flour
- 75g butter, cubed

To make the pastry, put the flour and butter in a large bowl. Rub the butter and flour together until it is mixed to the consistency of breadcrumbs. Make a well in the centre and use a knife to mix in 1 tablespoon of water. Gradually add another 2 tablespoons of water, mixing until it all comes together into a dough. I keep coaxing it together with the knife and then when it is almost all bound together I gather up the last bits by wiping the ball of dough around the bowl. Knead it gently to get it smooth, then flatten the ball and roll it out.

Chop the leeks into rounds, using most of the green part too. You can chop off the ends of the leeks and put them in your pot or bag for your next batch of stock, or freeze them for use in soup. Rinse the leeks well, making sure you get all the little bits of soil out that tend to lurk between the rings.

Sweat the leeks in the butter, then add to a 25cm pie dish along with your chicken and sweetcorn. I don't put pastry under the pie – only a pie crust on top. This is much easier as there's no danger of the infamous "soggy bottom". Pour over the white sauce, then cover with your pie crust, allowing it to overlap the top edge before trimming off the excess with a knife (the pastry will shrink a bit as it cooks). It's also nice to make Parmesan bites with your excess pastry (page 186).

Cook in the oven at 200°C/400°F/gas 6 for 35 to 40 minutes, or until piping hot and the pastry is golden.

Cottage Pie and Shepherd's Pie

Cottage pie is one of the ways we use up leftover roast beef from Sunday dinner. You can also use the same method to make shepherd's pie, swapping out the beef for lamb mince or leftover roast lamb and bulking it out with lentils, if you're short on meat. We get together with lots of family on a Sunday and it's our main meat day. I try to find out who's coming before I buy my joint of meat, but don't always manage it. Sunday is the day that if you're around you're welcome, so if we don't have a high ratio of meat to people we cook more roast potatoes and veg. If we have too much meat, then we'll have a plan for how to turn it into Monday's dinner.

Serves 4

- oil, for frying
- 1 onion, peeled and chopped
- 1 clove of garlic, peeled and finely chopped
- 1–2 stalks of celery or lovage with the leaves, chopped
- 400g minced beef or leftover roast beef, chopped in a food processor (supplement with corned beef, if necessary)
- leftover roast vegetables, such as peas, carrots, cabbage (or swap in frozen peas, a tin of sweetcorn or grated carrot)
- leftover gravy or chicken stock
- a dash of Worcestershire sauce
- leftover cooked potatoes
- a splash of milk and/or a knob of butter
- optional: a sprinkling of grated cheese

Heat a splash of oil in a large frying pan. Add the onion and sweat slowly until it starts to turn translucent, then add the garlic and celery or lovage.

Stir in the meat. If cooking from raw, cook for about 20 minutes until cooked through or warm through cooked beef until piping hot. When it's nearly there, add the veg to heat through.

Transfer to a deep ovenproof dish, add the gravy or stock and the Worcestershire sauce, mix together and season to taste with salt and pepper.

Mash the cooked potatoes with a little milk and butter, season with salt and pepper, then layer it over the meat. Sprinkle with grated cheese, if you like.

Put in the oven for around 20 minutes at 180°C/350°F/gas 4.

Bung-it-all-in Risotto

The secret of risotto is to add the liquid a bit at a time, allowing the rice to absorb it, then gradually add more, each time allowing the liquid to be almost fully absorbed. I will add liquid between 4 and 6 times. I usually have all kinds of rice in my store cupboard. I use white or brown short-grain rice. If using the brown short-grain rice you will need a longer cooking time and a bit more liquid and it will retain a slightly nutty texture.

Serves 4

- oil, for frying
- 1 onion, peeled and chopped
- 1 clove of garlic, peeled and finely chopped
- 1–2 stalks of celery or lovage with the leaves, chopped
- 1 leek, including most of the leaf, cut into rounds and washed thoroughly
- 260g white or brown short-grain rice
- 1.5 litres vegetable or chicken stock (page 169)
- leftover vegetables, such as peppers, leeks, tomatoes (don't worry if they're getting squidgy) and spring onions (for more ideas, see note)
- leftover cooked meat (I like to get all the meat from the underside of a roasted chicken, or that last slice of ham or bits of bacon or gammon)

Heat the oil in a large frying pan. Add the onion and sweat slowly until it starts to turn translucent, then add the garlic, celery or lovage and leek.

Add in the rice, swish it around in the pan for about 2 minutes, then add the first 150ml of stock and leave to simmer. You don't need to stir it constantly, just keep your eye on it and lift the rice off the bottom of the pan every now and then with a wooden spoon.

When the liquid is almost fully absorbed, add another 150ml of stock and leave to simmer until it's almost absorbed. Now, add the veg that takes longest to cook.

Repeat step 3 until you've used up your stock, gradually adding the veg according to how long it takes to cook, so veg like squash, carrots and parsnip will take longer than peppers or tomatoes. Stir in the meat before you add your last bit of stock so it heats up fully; around 15 minutes.

Keep going until the rice is cooked; for white rice about 35 minutes and brown rice about 55 minutes, but note you'll need more liquid.

NOTE: We love butternut squash and sage, with or without some feta cheese. Beetroot and feta (beware – it will be pink!) or mushrooms make great risotto too. Check out how Dean makes his on page 120.

Chicken and Mushroom Risotto

by Dean Pearce, @FoodRecycleDean

Dean says: "Over the years I've done quite a few presentations to schools – the future generation is so important in the long-term fight against food waste. I think we can get too hung up on perfection in cookery, but in my opinion – and what I try to tell the kids – is that it's great fun to experiment, to get inventive and sometimes get messy with food. I try to tell them not to be scared, but to have fun with it and get stuck in.

"I make risotto to use up mushrooms. It's also a great one for using up cream. Dead easy to make, but requires a bit of patience. I use chicken in this one, so start by frying the chicken in a nice big frying pan, browning it on all sides before removing to a separate plate for a few minutes. In the same pan, melt a couple of decent knobs of butter on a medium heat – you definitely don't want the pan too hot, patience is a virtue with risotto.

"Add some chopped onion and garlic and fry until soft, then add a bit more butter and allow to melt, so you've got a nice buttery garlicky onion base. Add the risotto rice (about 70g per person) stirring all the time. The rice should go translucent at the edges, but you don't want to brown it, just soften it for a few minutes in the butter and onions.

"Add a glass or two of white wine and boil for a few minutes to cook off the alcohol, again stirring all the time. Put the chicken back in the pan, add some mushrooms and give it a good stir.

"Now start adding the chicken stock. I usually make about 1 litre of it from about 500ml of chicken stock I've made at home (following a roast dinner) and the balance with 1 or 2 stock cubes and boiling water. Add the stock to the pan a bit at a time and keep stirring. The rice will start to soak up the liquid and expand. It's important to keep stirring to prevent the rice from sticking to the base of the frying pan. It also helps to release the starch, which naturally thickens the risotto.

"Keep adding the stock a bit at a time until the stock is all absorbed or the rice is tender and stodgy. Season to taste. Take it off the heat and add 100ml to 200ml of double cream, depending on how much you need to use up and how dry the risotto is. I think a risotto should be quite stodgy personally, but everyone has their own preference.

"The older mushrooms have bags of flavour, so a risotto is a great one for using them up. Of course, it's just as easy to make a vegetarian version without the chicken stock and chicken; mushrooms have great flavour and texture on their own."

Rogan Josh

When I was first married and we moved into a new house we used to say to friends that they could always call in on a Sunday and be promised a roast dinner. It was good practice for our family dinners on a Sunday now. It was back then that we started planning how to use up the meat to make meals for the rest of the week. Back then we used to buy a jar of sauce, but then we learnt to make the sauce ourselves.

Serves 4

- oil, for frying
- spices, such as mustard seeds, coriander seeds, cumin seeds, cayenne pepper, chilli seeds, chilli powder
- 1 onion, peeled and chopped
- 1 clove of garlic, peeled and finely chopped
- 1–2 stalks of celery or lovage with the leaves, chopped
- leftover cooked lamb, cubed (supplement with more veg, lentils or chickpeas)
- 1 tin of tomatoes
- leftover vegetables, such as peppers, leeks, squidgy tomatoes, spring onions
- rice, to serve

Heat the oil in a hob-safe casserole dish. Add any whole spices, such as mustard seeds or coriander seeds, and allow to pop, then add the onion and sweat slowly until it starts to turn translucent. Add the garlic and the celery or lovage and the remaining spices and cook for around 5 minutes.

Add in the lamb and swish it around in the pan for a couple of minutes, then pour in the tinned tomatoes. Swirl a splash of water around the tomato tin and add this too. Pop in your veg, then leave to simmer for 25 to 40 minutes, or until the meat is cooked and the flavours intensify – the longer you cook it, the more intense it will be.

If you make more than you need for your first meal, divide it into portions, leave to cool, then freeze it. It always tastes better the second time round. Defrost it overnight in the fridge, then heat through until piping hot (see chapter 3 for more about this). I quite often freeze mine in single portions with any leftover rice, so I have a lunch I can take out and about with me. I find a good home-cooked 'ready meal' is more satisfying than a sandwich.

Sweet and Sour Pork

by Helen McGonigal, spotofearth.com

Helen says: "This recipe is a great one to experiment with. I love looking in the cupboards and putting in a little bit of this or a little bit of that and seeing how it turns out. You can adapt it for any kind of meat too; it would work equally well with chicken or beef, or you could leave out the meat altogether and put in extra vegetables like courgettes, aubergines or any member of the squash family. It's great for using up all those bits of celery, peppers, onions and fruit that tend to linger in the fridge or fruit bowl."

Serves 4

- 1–2 tablespoons sesame oil (any oil will do, but sesame gives a nutty flavour)
- 500g diced pork (or chicken or beef, for slow cooking)
- 1 onion, peeled and chopped
- 1–2 sticks of celery, chopped
- 1 pepper, deseeded and chopped
- 3 spring onions, chopped
- 1 clove of garlic, crushed under a knife
- 2 teaspoons tom yum paste or shrimp paste or nam pla (fish sauce)
- 1 tablespoon marmalade
- 1 teaspoon salt
- ½ teaspoon ground Szechuan pepper
- 1 teaspoon each of ground ginger and crushed red chillies
- 1 tablespoon plain flour
- 2 satsumas, clementines or plums or 1 nectarine, peach or 1 small tin of mandarins
- juice of ½ a lime

Heat the oil in a hob-safe casserole or large sauté pan. Fry the pork, onion, celery, pepper, spring onions, garlic, tom yum, marmalade, salt and spices until the meat is browned all over.

Add the flour and stir until it's all mixed in. Pour over water to just cover, add the fruit and lime juice, then simmer for 1 to 2 hours until the pork is tender. If using chicken, cook for less time, or for beef you may need to simmer for a little longer.

The aim is to tick all the boxes of salty, sweet, sour and spicy, so taste the sauce and adjust it accordingly. For more spice increase the ginger and chillies or add a dash of chilli sauce. For more sweetness, add a little more fruit, marmalade or a teaspoon of brown sugar. For more saltiness, add a little more salt or more fish sauce, anchovy sauce, soy sauce or oyster sauce works well. For more sourness, add more lime juice. Experiment and enjoy! Serve with rice.

Pork Marsala

I have adapted this from my grandmother's recipe to use up roast pork.

Serves 4

- 1 onion, peeled and chopped
- 1 clove of garlic, peeled and finely chopped
- 2 stalks of celery and their leaves, finely chopped
- oil and/or butter, for frying
- 2 leeks, including plenty of green leaf, chopped into rings and washed thoroughly
- 400g raw minced pork or leftover cooked roast pork, minced
- fresh or dried mushrooms
- 400ml marsala wine, madeira or sherry

Pop the onion, garlic and celery into a large casserole dish with some oil or butter or a mix of both, then sweat gently. Add the leeks into the pan and continue sweating, until the onion is translucent.

Push the veg to the outside of the pan and brown the minced pork if cooking from raw or just add in the cooked pork and mix together.

If using dried mushrooms, rehydrate by soaking in boiling water (keep the soaking liquid). Chop the mushrooms and add to the pan, along with the soaking liquid, if using. Pour in the marsala wine, madeira or sherry, then bring to the boil.

Turn down the heat and simmer gently for 30 to 40 minutes. Season with salt and pepper, then serve with rice or baked potatoes.

A Pork Sandwich

Pork is one of my favourite cold meats to have as a sandwich. There was a bakery in Bourneville, where they sold a delicious pork bap. I wonder if it's still there? My clients moved away from Bourneville and so I no longer get the chance to visit, but I do make myself a nice pork sandwich when I have leftover roast pork.

The secret of the great pork sandwich is this: good bread. I make my own bread so I use that, but if you are buying bread, I would recommend the large floured white baps. You could keep some in your freezer. Add some stuffing and apple sauce if you have any leftover from Sunday dinner, otherwise add some chopped lettuce and mustard or chutney.

Simple and delicious!

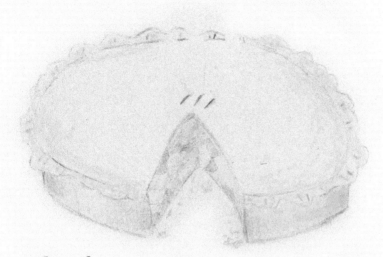

Making the most of your vegetables

Vegetable Chilli with Brown Rice and Cucumber Raita

by The Wiggly Worm, thewigglyworm.org.uk
Creating opportunities for life through food

The team at the Wiggly Worm says: *"The recipe we've included is something which works really well with the food surplus we receive. We can make this into a fantastic veggie chilli which we serve as part of our No Child Hungry Campaign here in Gloucestershire."*

Serves 4

For the chilli
- 1 tablespoon vegetable oil
- 1 medium onion, peeled and finely chopped
- 1 clove of garlic, peeled and finely chopped
- 3 mixed peppers, deseeded and diced
- 1 x 400g tin of butterbeans
- 1 x 400g tin of red kidney beans
- 1 x 400g tin of chopped tomatoes
- 1 teaspoon ground cinnamon
- 1 teaspoon cayenne pepper
- ½ teaspoon chilli powder
- 1 teaspoon ground cumin
- 200g brown rice
- 1 handful of fresh coriander

For the raita
- ½ cucumber
- 50ml plain yoghurt
- 3 tablespoons chopped mint
- 2 tablespoons lemon juice

Heat the oil in a pan, add the onion and sauté until soft. Add the garlic and peppers, drain and add the beans, then pour in the tomatoes. Simmer for 5 minutes.

Add the spices and stir. Simmer for 40 minutes or until the sauce has thickened. Bring a large pan of water to the boil and cook the brown rice.

To make the raita, peel and deseed the cucumber, before finely dicing. Combine all the ingredients in a bowl with a pinch of black pepper and mix.

Serve with the fresh coriander and raita on top of the chilli.

Broccoli Stalks with Houmous Dip

So many people discard the stalk of a head of broccoli. It is such a shame because it is so delicious and there are so many things you can do with it. One of my favourites is to have it as crudité (raw vegetables) with a houmous dip.

Serves 4 to 6 as a starter or snack

- 2 cloves of garlic, peeled and finely chopped
- 1 tin of chickpeas, drained
- 3 dessertspoons tahini
- juice of ½ a lemon
- 2 dessertspoons olive oil
- cayenne pepper (optional)
- broccoli stalks

Add all the ingredients (except the broccoli stalks) to a food processor or suitable bowl to use with a hand blender and whiz until smooth. Taste and add a little more lemon juice, tahini or chopped garlic, if you feel it needs it. You can sprinkle over a little cayenne pepper to serve to bring out the colours.

Peel the outer edge of the broccoli stalks (you can keep this to use in soup), then chop lengthways into fine strips for dipping into your houmous. Keep your houmous in a sealed container in the fridge and it should last for about 5 days. You can also freeze houmous and use it within 6 to 8 months.

Braised Cauliflower Leaves

The outer leaves of cauliflower are often needlessly thrown away, yet they can be a delicious addition to your meal. We often use them as a substitute for cabbage with our roast dinner.

- cauliflower leaves, roughly chopped like you'd chop cabbage
- a knob of butter
- black pepper

Steam for around 10 minutes. We then put them into a thermos dish that keeps your veg hot, along with the butter and a sprinkling of black pepper.

Potato Cakes

This was one of my great grandmother's recipes. My grandmother said they used to have them on a Sunday evening in the winter, sitting in front of the fire. I think they were popular in wartime, which is why her recipe is with margarine, but you can use butter if you prefer.

- flour
- margarine
- boiled, baked or roasted potatoes
- milk

Rub some flour and margarine together as if making pastry. Mash up the cooked potatoes or press them through a sieve, then mix it into the flour and margarine mixture. Add a drop of milk and press into a dough, then roll it out to about 1.5cm thickness, and using a cutter, stamp out your scones. Grill them for a few minutes each side or cook them on a hob in a dry frying pan, turning them over part way through cooking.

Re-fried Chip-Shop Chips

I do like the occasional treat of fish and chips, but we often seem to over-order on the chips. Fish and chips tends to be something we might pick up on the way back from a trip away. We used to have inconclusive and lengthy discussions about the portion sizes at the particular chip shop we were passing and could never get it right. Now we don't worry, as we know we will just freeze any leftovers and use them another time.

- chip-shop chips (straight from the freezer)
- oil (I use rapeseed oil) – enough to cover the bottom of your pan

Heat the oil in a large frying pan, then add the frozen chips. Stir and heat through until hot in the middle, then serve immediately. They're often better the second time round.

Middle-Eastern Style Lentil and Cabbage

from Good Food Oxford

Hannah Jacobs of Good Food Oxford says: "This recipe is from a vegetarian recipe swap we are running in North Oxford. This is part of a campaign with Low Carbon Oxford North to encourage the community to eat for health, planet and taste buds by eating less meat and experimenting with veg. The recipe is from North Oxford resident Rebecca Nestor."

Serves 1 generously

- 100g red lentils
- 1 fresh red or green chilli pepper, finely chopped
- 1 preserved lemon, finely chopped
- ½ tin of tomatoes
- 100g Savoy cabbage, finely chopped
- 1 tablespoon freshly grated ginger
- 1 teaspoon turmeric (dried or puréed in a jar. Fresh turmeric is lovely but it's usually air-freighted)
- 1 tablespoon dukkah (an Egyptian mix of herbs, nuts and spice)

Cook the lentils, along with the chilli, lemon and tomatoes, according to the packet instructions until tender and the liquid has absorbed.

Stir-fry the cabbage for 2 to 3 minutes with the ginger and turmeric. Turn the lentils out into a bowl, top with the cabbage, sprinkle the dukkah on top and eat with a spoon.

Leon's Pumpkin with Leeks and Sage

from Good Food Oxford

Hannah says: "This recipe is from our Pumpkin Rescue. Since its launch in Oxford in 2014, Pumpkin Rescue has taken the UK by storm. For Halloween 2016, Pumpkin Rescue was taken on by 25 UK towns and even crossed oceans to the USA and Asia. So far, Pumpkin Rescue has delivered 199 local events and 12,200 people have attended workshops, from which a whopping 17,000 pumpkins were diverted from landfill."

Serves 4 as a side dish

- 500g pumpkin, peeled
- 2 tablespoons olive oil
- 1 red onion, peeled and sliced
- 5 fresh sage leaves, shredded
- 4 leeks, finely sliced into rounds
- 1 tablespoon balsamic vinegar
- optional: Parmesan cheese

Preheat the grill or a griddle pan. Finely slice the pumpkin, then place into a bowl and toss with 1 tablespoon of olive oil. Season well with salt and freshly ground black pepper, then grill for a few minutes on each side.

Heat the rest of the oil in a large pan. Cook the onion and sage leaves for 5 minutes over a medium heat. Season, then add the leeks and cook for a further 5 minutes, stirring well. Stir in the balsamic vinegar and remove from the heat.

Arrange the pumpkin slices on a large serving dish and top with the onion and leeks. You can also add some Parmesan slivers, if you like.

THE SCARY TRUTH ABOUT PUMPKINS

42% of people buy pumpkins in the UK each year, but they don't always end up in a happy home:

25% throw it in the bin as food waste.

19% add it to the compost heap.

33% cook the edible pumpkin they carve out.

20% put it in food waste collection.

A whopping 18,000 tonnes of pumpkin are thrown away each year. That's the same as 360 million portions of pumpkin pie.

= 360 million portions of pumpkin pie.

JOIN THE #PUMPKINRESCUE! FIND YOUR LOCAL EVENT AT WWW.HUBBUB.ORG.UK

There are many more ways to eat your pumpkin. Find and share recipes on social media with #PUMPKINRESCUE

Buttered Radishes with Caraway

by Tom Hunt, author of The Natural Cook (Quadrille)

Tom says: "This is a good recipe if your radishes are a little old. Wash the radishes well. If the radishes have tops, cut them off, shred the stalks and leaves and put to one side."

- 100g radishes and leaves (optional)
- a knob of butter
- a pinch of caraway
- a few sprigs of fresh flat-leaf parsley, leaves picked

Wash and cut the radishes into halves, or quarters if they are really big. Place the butter in a heavy-based frying pan and bring to a medium heat. Add the radishes and cook slowly for 3 minutes till their pink colours dull slightly and bleed into the flesh. Be careful the pan doesn't get too hot, otherwise the butter will burn.

Add the radish leaves (if you have them), caraway, a sprinkle of salt and pepper and cook for a further 30 seconds to allow the aromas to come to life. Serve tossed with parsley leaves.

Radish Leaf Soup with Caraway

by Tom Hunt, author of The Natural Cook (Quadrille)

Tom says: "This dish is shockingly good. A great thrifty use of the leaves and a simple recipe to make. I like to thicken it with risotto rice as it gives the soup a velvety texture and is a nice break from floury potatoes."

Serves 4

- 1 onion, peeled and finely sliced
- 3 cloves of garlic, peeled and roughly chopped
- 1 small courgette, roughly diced
- green top of a leek, roughly sliced
- 1 stick celery, roughly sliced
- 1 bay leaf
- 2 sprigs of fresh mint
- 1 quantity of buttered radishes (see recipe above)
- 50g risotto rice or short-grain brown rice
- 150g radish leaves and/or watercress
- extra radish and butter, to serve

Sauté the onion, garlic, courgette, leek, celery, bay leaf and mint stalks (pick the leaves and set aside) for 10 minutes on a low heat.

Add 700ml of water, the buttered radishes and rice. Bring to the boil and simmer for 25 minutes till the rice is soft.

Add the radish tops and/or watercress and the mint leaves, then blend until smooth and a vibrant green. Serve with grated radish and a little knob of butter on top.

The soup will lose some of its green vibrancy but will keep fine for 3 days in the fridge. The buttered radishes are best fresh.

Buttered radishes with rare beef are delicious: cook a portion of beef steak with the radishes and caraway for 3 minutes, then slice thinly and serve together with the brown butter. Or try radish and anchovy butter. If you have any spare radishes, grate them and combine with butter. Add salt and a sprinkle of caraway and serve on toasts.

133

Cauliflower Steak, Mushroom and Lemon Thyme

By Douglas McMaster @mcmasterchef, Silo restaurant, Silobrighton.com

Douglas says: "This is a vegan game changer: its robust meaty quality will convert the most resilient of carnivores. The beauty of the cauliflower 'tree of life' presentation makes it the ultimate dinner party showstopper."

Serves 4 to 6

For the cauliflower steak
- 3 medium to large cauliflowers

For the mushroom risotto
- 600g button mushrooms
- soy sauce (optional)
- 300g short grain brown rice
- 100g lemon thyme
- 50g brown rice miso paste

- There will be a lot of cauliflower trim, this is ideal for a salad, soup or a vegan cauliflower curry
- The mushroom stock leaches all the flavour from the mushroom. The actual mushrooms can be used to thicken a soup or go into a curry for nice chunky texture - zero waste
- The lemon thyme can take a little bit of time to pick
- Ideally your serving plate will be slightly concave. If it's flat the mushroom stock/sauce will run across the plate. Heat the plates up before service

Mushroom risotto

The stock should be your first job as it takes about an hour. Roughly slice your mushrooms and sweat in rapeseed oil at a high heat, in a heavy based pan. Cook until golden brown. Then add 2 litres of water, bring to a simmer and leave for 40–50 minutes until it tastes very mushroomy. Strain off your mushroom slices to use in another dish.

Reduce the mushroom liquid until it tastes quite intense. Season with soy to make it even more intense. It needs to be very strong as the rice and cauliflower are quite neutral flavours.

Meanwhile boil your short grain brown rice for about 20 minutes until it starts to break down and is very tender to eat. Strain and reserve ready for your service.

Cauliflower

Take all the outer leaves off the cauliflower and reserve for another use (e.g. see page 129). Turn the head of cauliflower upside down and cut directly down through the centre of the root. Then cut the steak 2 ½cm from the centre, parallel with your first cut. This will reveal a beautiful 'tree of life' steak. You will get 2 big steaks from 1 cauliflower. Reserve all the cauliflower trim for another use (e.g. the soup on page 192).

Bring a suitably sized pan of water to a simmer. Season the water, it should taste slightly salty. To be really precise, the salt should be 5% weight of the water. Poach the steaks until tender. This can be done ahead of time.

Lemon thyme

Pick your lemon thyme into individual leaves, this is a slow job and can be done whenever you have a spare 10 mins, perhaps when your rice and mushroom stock are doing their business. If your stalks are available after picking, throw them into the mushroom stock for extra flavour.

To serve

- Put your rice in a heavy based pot with half of your mushroom liquid and season with the brown rice miso paste. Gently warm but don't boil, the more you beat this mixture the more glutinous the risotto will become.
- Warm the steaks up in a steamer or neatly lay them into a pan with a lid on and a small amount of water, until they are hot.
- Spoon about 3 large tablespoons of risotto into the base of each (hot) plate. Ideally the plate will be slightly concave so to neatly capture the mushroom stock/sauce
- Sprinkle the lemon thyme leaves around the edges of the risotto
- Place the steaks neatly on the centre of the risotto
- Finish by neatly drizzling the remains of the mushroom stock/sauce around the edge of the risotto.

Voilà...

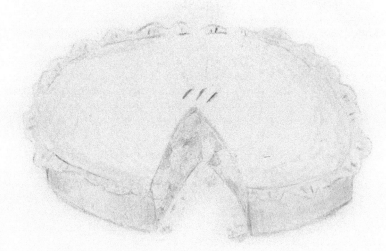

Using up the glut from the garden and hedgerows

Rhubarb and Apple Jam

by Vicky Owen blogging as busygreenmum

Vicky says: "Rhubarb is easy to grow and generally provides a large crop. Ours grows so well in its spot next to the compost bin that we always have more than we know what do with during late spring/early summer. Preserving it in a jam is a great way of keeping some for later in the year (although I must admit to eating this straight away). Although best made with early rhubarb you can also use larger stalks just fine. Our rhubarb plant has been passed down through the generations so I have no idea what variety it is – it originally came from a plant in my great grandfather's garden and as a child it came with us when we moved house. When I first got my own place we split the plant so I could plant my own and it has since moved again with me, and a plant has been returned to my father for his allotment.

"I have suggested adding apples in this recipe but you can leave them out or substitute other fruit – rhubarb and strawberry is a good combination. You could also add elderflowers which should become available while there is still plenty of rhubarb – you would infuse approx 10 flower heads (best picked on a dry day and shaken to remove insects rather than washed) wrapped in a muslin or tea towel at step 1 below and then removed before cooking the jam."

- 1kg rhubarb stalks, washed and trimmed, then sliced into 1cm chunks
- 1kg preserving sugar
- 1 lemon
- 1teaspoon ground ginger (optional)
- 2 or 3 small eating apples, peeled, cored and cut into small pieces. (you could substitute a larger cooking apple)
- 25g unsalted butter

Equipment needed:

- Large bowl
- Either a preserving pan or a heavy based large saucepan
- Wooden spoon
- Grater or lemon zester
- Sterilised jars – you can reuse old jam jars
- Jam or sugar thermometer (optional) or put several saucers in the fridge or freezer (to use later to test the jam setting point).

This recipe will probably make about 5 or 6 jars depending on the size but I usually have a few more ready just in case. To sterilise you should wash them thoroughly in soapy water or a dishwasher and dry in an oven at 140°C for at least 10 minutes – then keep them warm until ready to use. Scald the clean lids in boiling water. You can alternatively use a sterilising solution and warm the jars after rinsing thoroughly.

Place the sliced rhubarb into a large bowl with the sugar. Use the lemon zester or grater to grate the lemon rind into the bowl. Then cut the lemon in half and squeeze in the juice.

Give it all a stir. Cover the bowl with a clean cloth such as a tea towel and leave for a few hours, stirring occasionally. You should see some juices start to come out of the rhubarb (if not you can leave it longer – some recipes say to leave overnight but I find just a few hours works fine).

Meanwhile wash and sterilise your jars.

Empty your bowl of rhubarb and sugar with all the juices into your pan. Add the chopped apple and ginger (if using). Bring the mixture to a boil slowly so that the rhubarb and apple have time to soften.

Then bring the mix to a rolling boil and boil until it reaches setting point, stirring frequently to prevent sticking. I found this took about 20 minutes but this may vary.

How to test for setting point

The setting point should be achieved at around 104–105°C. However you may find it difficult to test accurately if you are making a relatively small amount of jam in a large pan – I have never managed it and prefer the saucer method. When you think the jam is approaching setting point (it will start to thicken a little), get a cold saucer from your fridge/freezer and carefully drop a little of the jam onto it. Give it a moment to cool and then press with your finger – if ready it should wrinkle a little. If not cook for another few minutes and test again.

Once your jam has reached setting point remove from the heat, stir in the butter, and leave to cool down a little. You may find it has formed a skin on cooling in which case give it a quick stir before spooning carefully into your warmed jars. Place the lids on while still warm.

Image: Vicky Owen

Ratatouille

This is a great recipe to use up all that summer veg from your fridge or to use up any glut of veg from your garden.

Makes 4 to 6 portions

* 1 onion
* 1 tablespoon of rapeseed oil
* 2 cloves of garlic
* 6–10 fresh tomatoes, chopped or 1–2 tins of chopped tomatoes
* a vegetable glut, such as courgettes, marrow, peppers and aubergine

Chop the onion and sweat in a little oil, then squash or finely chop the garlic and add to the pan along with the tomatoes.

Chop the peppers, courgettes, aubergines, marrows; you can use any combination of these vegetables in any quantity. I suggest about 150 grammes of veg per portion. If you are going for nearer 6 portions use 2 tins of tomatoes. Add the chopped veg to the pan and allow it to heat through until softened.

If you don't want to use all your ratatouille straight away you can freeze once cooled. I usually freeze it in portions as it's ideal for a low-calorie lunch on its own or as a vegetable accompaniment.

Chilli Oil

Chillies are easy to grow in a pot on your windowsill. If you have a glut of chillies or even just buy more than you need from a supermarket, you can finely chop the chillies and store then in an ice cube tray in the freezer. Alternatively, you might like to make some chilli oil.

* olive oil
* fresh or dried chillies
* garlic, peeled
* dried chillies and other dried herbs for decoration

Pour the olive oil into a saucepan and heat gently. Add your fresh chillies and garlic and allow them to infuse. Cook on a gentle heat for 20 minutes to get a good chilli heat into the oil. Strain the oil into a sterilised bottle or jar.

You don't add the fresh chillies or garlic into the jar but you can add in a couple of dried chillies for decoration. You can add dried sprigs of rosemary and black peppercorns for both added taste and beauty.

Spinach or Chard with Poached Egg

When I was growing up we kept chickens for a while. In springtime we had an abundance of leafy spinach and fresh eggs, so this really did feel like a 'free lunch'. When you keep your own chickens, you soon learn about the egg test. Pop the eggs in a bowl of water; if they sink to the bottom they are still fresh, but if they float on top, throw them on the compost heap and run.

Serves 2

- 200g spinach leaves, washed and roughly chopped
- a knob of butter
- a pinch of nutmeg
- 1 or 2 eggs per person

Steam the spinach for about 10 minutes, then drain well. Add the butter, a pinch of nutmeg and a generous twist or several of black pepper and keep warm. Poach the eggs in water and serve on top of the spinach. Delicious!

Blackberry and Apple Crumble

This is an excellent autumn pudding, made with free blackberries from the hedge and the windfall apples from our tree.

Serves 6

- 75g butter
- 150g plain flour
- 100g oats
- 50g sugar
- 500g blackberries and sliced apples

Rub the butter into the flour until it looks like breadcrumbs. Then stir in the oats and the sugar. Place your blackberries and apple slices in the bottom of your dish and spread out the crumble mixture over the top. Bake in the oven at 190°C/375°F/gas 5 for around 40 minutes until the crumble topping is golden brown.

It is delicious served with custard or with ice cream.

Chutney Challenge

by Jenny Costa, Rubies in the Rubble

Jenny says: "If you have never made chutney before, I'd love to challenge you. Making chutney is an amazingly satisfying process: from finding the best recipe, sourcing the ingredients and mixing them all together to labelling the jars, lining them up, and dolloping a spoonful on a cracker.

"Chutney can spice up the most lacklustre of sandwiches, salads or leftovers! There are hundreds of combinations of ingredients for chutney – most have a fruit base but many vegs can be used too. The basic composition of any chutney is fruit/veg, spices, sugar and vinegar and then it's as simple as chopping them all up and throwing everything in a pot.

"Chutneys come under the heading of 'preserve' which seems like quite an austere, old-fashioned word, but they are really straightforward and fun to make. Images of enormous vats bubbling away can be a little daunting but it can be as simple as 'I have some apples, a bit of spice, tomatoes and onions lying around, let's make chutney!'

"The great thing about chutney is that there is endless potential for experimentation. Once you have the basic concept you can experiment with all sorts of ingredients: bananas, mangos, apples, nectarines, apricots, tomatoes, rhubarb, dried fruits or a combination of all of them. You can use almost any fruit or vegetable, and different combinations of spices.

"Autumn is the traditional time, at the end of the harvest, while people stocked up for the winter months ahead, to make preserves that would keep food interesting. Therefore many chutney recipes are based on autumnal fruit and veg – a quick search online will give you an idea to get going on some and creating your own in no time."

Before you start, here are some really basic golden rules that I would advise you stick to:

- Chop veg roughly the same size so that everything cooks at the same time. If you shred your fruit and veg too fine, you'll end up with spicy puree; but too chunky and you'll end up with half an onion falling out of your cheese and pickle sandwich. Daintily chopped vegetables can transform a good chutney into a brilliant one.

- The ratio of fruit/vegetables to vinegar and sugar will vary depending on the sweetness and acidity of the fruit and vegetables. Sweet vegetables, such as carrots, or fruit, such as dates, will need less sugar. With acidic tomatoes you can hold back on the vinegar. As a very basic ratio 3kg vegetables/fruit to 1 litre vinegar and 500g sugar, then adjust for taste. The rough ratio is: fruit, vinegar; sugar 6:2:1.

- Put all your ingredients in a large saucepan, and heat gently, stirring the mix until the sugar has dissolved, then bring to the boil, turn the

heat down again and simmer. Many recipes state a time but this can vary hugely depending on ripeness and the fruit or veg you are working with. A good way of knowing when it's a good consistency, is to pull a spoon through your chutney and it should leave a line behind it.

- Sterilise jars by running them through a dishwasher cycle, or washing them with hot soapy water and placing in an oven at 100°C for 10–15 mins.

- Fill with the warm chutney, pressing down well. Half screw on the lids until the jars are cool: then it is OK to tighten. Chutneys are best left to mature for a couple of months before eating because the acids from the vinegar soften and the fruit flavours have time to meld and become more complex.

Zero Food Miles Salad

by Wendy Shillam, www.rooftopvegplot.com

Wendy says: "No waste and simple. The fresher the produce the better it tastes."

Every lunch time in the summer I go round the 'rooftopvegplot' with a salad shaker and a pair of scissors snipping salad leaves, herbs and edible flowers. I gently wash the salad then tip it into a bowl and dress with a vinaigrette (I keep a pre-mixed bottle in the writing hut) season with homemade celery salt*.

It's delicious and nutritious. And different every day. Little and often will encourage the plant to grow more leaves for next week's lunches.

Typical content:

- lettuce of every hue and style
- Chinese leaves
- chard
- young spinach leaves
- nasturtium (leaves and flowers)
- mustard leaves
- borage
- mint
- parsley
- chives
- sage
- hyssop
- wild celery
- marigold
- lavender
- dill

* To make celery salt pound sea salt in a pestle and mortar with the seeds of wild celery. Keep in an airtight spice jar in the dark.

Nettle Pesto

by Wendy Graham, moralfibres.co.uk

Wendy says: "We have a patch of wild nettles in our garden that we keep for the ladybirds. If you don't have a patch of nettles in your garden then its really easy to forage for wild nettles. There are a couple of plants that look like nettles, such as the False Nettle and Horse Balm, so do make sure you're not in any doubt about what you're picking. I found a handy guide to identifying nettles that you might find useful if you're not 100% sure. I felt quite confident as we've had our patch of nettles for over four years now, and I've been stung a few times on them whilst gardening!

"To avoid getting stung whilst harvesting your nettles for the pesto wear long sleeves and gloves, and arm yourself with a pair of scissors and a container. To pick the nettles just cut the young leaves at the top of the stem – you don't want the big old leaves and thick stems. Give the leaves a shake before you put them in your container to remove any insects that might be on the leaves. And lastly, try not to pick beside paths where dogs might have widdled on them!

"Wild nettle pesto is definitely a spring-time delicacy – make sure you pick your nettles before they flower as flowering nettles can upset your urinary tract if consumed. You are you should be ok until late May.

"Wild nettle pesto is really delicious stirred into pasta, in omelettes, on sandwiches, on pizzas, or incorporated into other recipes. It's also super quick and easy to make – it takes less than 15 minutes to whip up. It tastes not too dissimilar to spinach pesto, and don't worry, nettles lose their sting after being cooked, so there's no chance of being stung! I loosely adapted this recipe and added chilli for an extra tasty kick."

- 1 handful of freshly picked nettles
- 45g pinenuts
- 4 raw cloves of garlic
- 45g of vegetarian hard cheese (grated) (I used Twineham Grange hard cheese which is Vegetarian Society approved. If you're not vegetarian then any hard cheese, such as parmesan or grana padano can be used)
- ½ teaspoon of salt
- ½ teaspoon of pepper
- 10ml of lemon juice
- ¼ teaspoon of chilli flakes (or more or less depending on your taste)
- 140ml of olive oil

Wash your nettles, and bring a large pot of salted water (just a pinch) to boil. When the water is boiling add your nettles to the pot and boil for two minutes.

Remove your nettles from the pot and place in a bowl of cold water.

Toast your pine nuts in a dry pan (no oil) until golden brown.

Add the nuts to your food processor, and add your cloves of garlic, grated hard cheese, salt, pepper and lemon juice (and chilli flakes if you're using them). Pulse for a minute or two until you have a grainy texture.

Remove your nettles from the cold water and squeeze out as much water as you can. I place my nettles in an old tea towel, twist it up, and wring it out to remove the excess water, but you can do it by hand as the nettles don't sting after boiling.

Add your nettles to the food processor, and pulse the mixture for a minute until it's green and grainy.

Whilst your food processor is still running slowly drizzle in the olive oil until the pesto is quite gloopy. You may end up using more or less olive oil than 140ml depending on what your preferred consistency is.

Transfer the pesto to a sterilised jar and store in the fridge for up to 1 week. Use as you would any pesto.

Zingy Orange, Rosemary and Honey Infused Water

by Christina McDermott, Relish, relishcommunity.com

Christina says: "A refreshing cool drink for a long summer's days, and a great way to use your rosemary trimmings."

Makes 4 standard size glasses

- 1 litre water
- juice of 2 blood oranges or 100ml orange juice
- 3 fresh sprigs of rosemary, finely chopped
- 3 teaspoons of honey

In a jug, pour in the water and orange juice and stir. Add the rosemary. Stir in the honey,

For best results leave this to stand covered at room temperature for a couple of hours.

Serve with ice – refreshment on the rocks!

Aromatic Elderflower and Ginger Cordial

by Susanne Austin

Susanne says: "Elderflower come into blossom at the end of May/beginning of June. We have a window of opportunity for around 3 to 4 weeks to look for flower heads that are in full bloom and as full of as much pollen as possible – which is just how we want them.

"It is best to pick on a hot sunny day so that plant is sun drenched and dry – as well as picking blossom high in the tree so as to avoid soiled blooms at lower points of the tree.

"When foraging be sure that you have correct permissions to pick/harvest that which you are picking/harvesting. Be mindful of the land you pass through and be respectful toward the tree/shrub/bush and/or plant itself. In the case of elderflowers leaving some heads on the tree to allow the plant to set berries and seeds because we will want to return to them in the autumn to gather berries for elderberry recipes such as elderberry jelly or wine.

"When picking Elderflower blooms only pick the flower heads, leaving the leaves and branches behind, thus causing no damage to the tree.

"Elderflower is anti-viral, anti-bacterial and has anti catarrh properties, making it a natural medicine. As Hippocrates, the father of medicine, would say - "Let food be thy medicine and medicine be thy food" and even Mrs Beeton advised on the beneficial properties of elderflower wine!"

You will need:
- elderflower heads, a basket full (around 30 heads) minus leaves, stalks and insects
- 1.7 litres water
- 4 lemons, unwaxed, finely grated for zest then sliced
- 2 oranges, unwaxed, finely grated for zest then sliced
- 7cm piece fresh ginger, grated
- ¾ tablespoon of ginger preserve
- 900g sugar elixir or 900g granulated sugar

For the sugar elixir use:
- 225g granulated sugar
- 225g Total Sweet Xylitol (a natural sugar alternative)
- 225g demerara sugar (unrefined raw cane sugar)
- 225g raw honey

Remove all insects and stems from elderflower heads. Do not wash as this removes the pollen. Place elderflower heads in ceramic bowl or plastic bucket.

Boil the water in a pan with all the other ingredients until sugar and honey are fully dissolved. Pour the liquid over the elderflower heads, mix, cover with a clean tea towel and leave to stand for 24 hours.

To bottle – you will need:

- a ceramic or glass bowl
- a colander or strainer
- a muslin cloth or tea towel
- a jug
- sterilised bottles

To sterilize bottles, place cleaned/washed bottles onto racks in a cold oven. Turn oven on to 160ºC/320ºF/gas 3. Leave bottles in the oven until 10 minutes after it has reached temperature then turn off leaving bottles in the oven to cool.

Place a colander or strainer into the glass bowl placing the muslin inside the colander/strainer. Pour steeped liquid into the centre of the muslin cloth to strain.

Pour the cordial into the jug and from the jug into the bottles, filling bottles to the brim so as to minimise air at the top. Seal tightly, label and date.

The elderflower and ginger cordial will last for around 3 to 6 months. The bottles are best stored in a dark cupboard, then put in the fridge once opened.

You can also make your elderflower and ginger cordial into ice lollies, ice cubes or freeze in larger batches in freezer bags.

Whether made with cool still or fizzy mineral water, the taste is simply divine and the aromatic scent an intoxicating and natural delight.

Wild Garlic Bread

by Ian Cumming, Great British Bake Off finalist ianbakes.com

Makes 1 loaf

- 40g unsalted butter
- 500g strong white flour
- 10g instant yeast
- 10g fine sea salt
- 100g fairly finely chopped wild garlic leaves
- 75g finely grated parmesan
- 300ml just warm water

Rub the butter into the flour in a large mixing bowl. Add the yeast, salt, garlic leaves, parmesan and the warm water. (I find 300ml tap water warmed for 50 seconds in a microwave gives a good temperature.) Different flours require slightly different amounts of water so you may need to add a wee bit more flour or water depending on the texture but you should be aiming for a smooth, elastic dough.

If kneading by hand you may find it easier with a large spoon or fork at first before getting your hands stuck in. If using a mixer then use the dough hook and knead on slow at first for a couple of minutes before increasing the speed to medium. Either way knead for several minutes.

Place the dough in a large oiled mixing bowl. Cover and leave it to rest for an hour or two in a warm spot in the house.

Once it has doubled in size, knock it back by briefly kneading again. Maybe it is because of the cheese in the dough but I find it can stick to the side of my usual loaf tin so I line the tin with baking parchment before putting in the dough. Allow it to more or less double in size again.

Preheat the oven to 220°C/475°F/gas 7. Dust the top of the loaf with some extra flour and then bake for about 20 minutes before turning down to 180°C/350°F/gas 4 for another 10–20 minutes.

Turn out and leave to cool. Almost all bread is gorgeous when it is still warm from the oven but a slice of this one slathered with some salty butter is on another level!

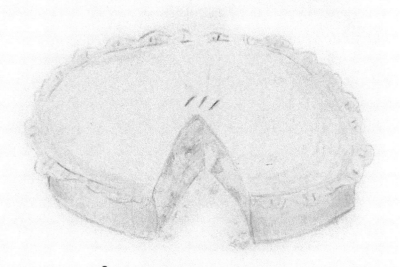

Loving your leftovers

Egg and Vegetable Fried Rice

by Cyrus Todiwala, Cafe Spice Namaste

Cyrus says: "There are millions of Chinese people in India who form a part of the Indian people now. Chinese food in India was perhaps more popular in restaurants than Indian food until very recently. The Indian Chinese have developed their own distinct cuisine due simply to the Indian palate demanding the food to be different, having evolved from the provinces of Sichuan, Hunan or Hakka. I am giving a very simple fried rice preparation, which is ideal with leftover boiled rice."

Serves 2 to 3

- 2 to 3 tablespoons oil
- 2 eggs, well beaten
- 3 spring onions, sliced at an angle
- 1 small green pepper, finely sliced into strips (or swap in a mixture of colours)
- 500g leftover boiled rice (use old or freshly boiled rice, well drained and cooled. The rice must be cold, so refrigerate after boiling. 150g uncooked rice will make about 500g cooked rice)
- mixed vegetables, blanched and finely diced (or use shredded carrot, fine beans, diced mushrooms and green peas)
- light or dark soy sauce

Heat the oil in a wok over a high heat until smoking. Add the beaten egg and swirl with a ladle or spoon breaking it up as you go.

Add the spring onions and peppers and sauté for a minute over a high heat. Add the vegetables and a pinch of salt and pepper and sauté for a minute or so, stirring and tossing from time to time. Add the rice and toss gently until heated through. If you don't know how to toss with a wok, use the frying spoon.

Season with salt and pepper and a dash or few of soy sauce – be careful if using dark soy. Taste and serve.

Dead Bread Pudding

by Jen Gale, My Make Do and Mend Life

Jen says: "I love this recipe as it's such a great way of using up all the leftover bits and pieces of bread that somehow inevitably seem to just happen, despite my best efforts. My kids are still quite young and have an annoying habit of leaving their toast crusts, or only half-eating sandwiches and rolls. I simply scoop all the leftover bits (fillings, spread and all) into a bag in the freezer, and when I have enough I can throw together this easy savoury bread pudding. It is good comfort food for tea on cold winter evenings and goes down a storm with baked beans on the side. Any leftovers are also pretty good cold for lunch the next day!"

Serves 4

- 400–500g dead bread
- 600ml milk
- 2 eggs, beaten
- grated cheese, wholegrain mustard, sautéed onions (optional)

Bung your dead bread (frozen or otherwise) into a mixer and blitz into breadcrumbs (you can omit this stage if you want). Mix together the milk and beaten eggs in a jug, then pour it over the bread chunks and leave to soak for a bit.

Grease a baking tray (I use our brownie tray, which measures 20cm x 15cm), pour in the mixture, then top with grated cheese if you like that sort of thing (and frankly, who doesn't?). Preheat the oven if you feel the need, or just whack it all in cold, then turn on the oven and cook for a few minutes longer. Cook for about 45 minutes at 180°C/350°F/gas 4.

Panzanella

from Sara Green, Derby Food Assembly

Sara says: "This recipe is a fantastic way of using up leftover stale bread."

- 4–5 handfuls of stale bread
- 5–6 tablespoons olive oil
- 1 tablespoon red wine vinegar
- 6 tomatoes, sliced
- 1 cucumber, sliced
- 1 medium red onion, peeled (keep the peel for your stock pot)
- 3 cloves of garlic, peeled and finely chopped (keep peel for your stock pot)
- fresh basil leaves

Season the bread with salt and pepper, then add the olive oil and the red wine vinegar. Slice and add the tomatoes, cucumber and onion to the bread. Stir in the garlic. Mix well.

Add more red wine vinegar to taste, then serve with fresh basil.

Use-it-up Tuna, Runner Bean and Kohlrabi Lasagne

by Zoe Morrison, ecothriftyliving.com

Zoe says: "Don't worry if you don't have runner beans or kohlrabi, just get creative with what you have!"

Serves 4

- 1–2 tins of tuna
- 1 small spoonful of horseradish sauce
- several large runner beans, chopped into pieces
- a batch of tomato sauce
- dried lasagne sheets
- ¼–½ of a kohlrabi, thinly sliced
- a batch of white sauce (see page 197)
- grated cheese (optional)

Grease an appropriate-sized baking dish for your lasagne. Mix the tuna, horseradish sauce and chopped runner beans together with the tomato sauce.

Put a sheet of lasagne at the bottom of the dish, followed by a layer of tuna and tomato sauce, and a layer of kohlrabi. If you don't have kohlrabi, you can replace it with whatever you like, such as squash, turnip or aubergine.

Next add a layer of white sauce and grate over some cheese, if using. Add another layer of lasagne and repeat until you have run out of space. Finish off with a layer of lasagne topped with white sauce, then cover with grated cheese.

Bake in the oven for 1 hour at 180°C/350°F/gas 4.

Keep an eye on it as you may want to turn the heat down a little or cover the lasagne after around half an hour to prevent it from burning. You could probably also cook it for a shorter time if you're in a hurry. Once ready serve hot and enjoy with greens.

Pasta and Bolognese Leftover Pie

Brian Turner CBE, brianturner.co.uk

Brian says: "I chose this recipe as I often have pasta and Bolognese leftover when feeding my wonderful grandchildren so it works well."

- butter
- shortcrust pastry
- 4 tomatoes, chopped
- 1 onion, peeled and finely chopped
- 350g leftover cooked minced meat
- 170g leftover cooked pasta, chopped
- 1 egg, beaten
- puff pastry
- garlic

Grease an enamelled pie dish with butter. Roll out the shortcrust pastry slightly larger than the size of your dish, then lay it over, pressing it into the sides and leaving the pastry overhanging. Bake for 20 minutes in the oven at 180°C/350°F/gas 4. Trim to shape and cool.

Melt 30g of butter in a pan, add the chopped tomatoes, onion and garlic and cook for 5 minutes. Add the minced meat, stir well, then add the pasta. Season and allow to cool.

Spoon into the cooked tart case, brush the edges with beaten egg, then roll out the puff pastry so it's a little larger than the dish. Push down to seal, brush the top with egg.

Bake for 40 minutes at 180°C/350°F/gas 4.

City Harvest Super Hash

Adam Svoboda, City Harvest London

Adam says: "At City Harvest we love American-style hash: a scrumptious mix of diced potatoes, well seasoned and combined with a load of other diced veggies and, if you like, meat. The flavours combine beautifully and the dish pan-fries up to a crispy, comforting perfection, ideal with a couple of fried eggs for a lazy Sunday breakfast, or a little salad for a quick and hearty midweek dinner.

"We also love this dish's flexibility: you only need a single skillet to make it, and once you've got the basic idea down, the sky is the limit as far as ingredients – it works with almost any veg or meat.

"This makes it not only the tastiest way we know of to clear leftovers and tired looking stuff out the fridge, but one of the most efficient!"

There are a few little tricks to making great hash.

You want to cook with relatively high heat (medium-high) and scrape the pan every once in a while with a spatula to free up and incorporate the crispy brown bits that form on the bottom. These bits add an incredible layer of flavour to the finished product. This is the secret of great hash!

If things start to burn, just knock down the heat a bit, stir more frequently, or add a little splash of water or stock to the pan.

Add veggies to the pan one at a time, not all at once. Adding slower-cooking stuff (like potatoes) first and quicker-cooking stuff (like peas) later will help ensure everything gets cooked evenly. Try to keep all the chopped veggies about the same size so they cook at about the same rate – particularly the harder stuff like root vegetables.

The recipe here is enough for 2 very hungry people to stuff themselves – or for 3 lighter eaters. Any root veg or aromatic will work great – leafy greens not so much (they tend to break down too much during cooking). Likewise, any meat, cooked or uncooked, can be minced, chopped, shredded, or crumbled in. Potatoes are really the only "must have" ingredient, so once you get the basic technique, feel free to go to town with substitutions, omissions or additions, and make this dish your own!

Serves 2 to 3

- 6–7 big potatoes (any variety), peeled
- 2 carrots, peeled
- 3 celery stalks, trimmed
- 1 onion (white or red)

- garlic (to taste)
- meat of any type, cooked or uncooked. We love to use chorizo.
- a couple of cups of water or stock
- oil, for cooking
- salt, pepper – paprika also works well
- herbs (fresh or dried) if desired
- egg or a bit of salad (to serve with the hash)

Dice up the potatoes and carrots into cubes between 1–2 cm but no bigger – the smaller you go, the better things will cook and the more of those magical little crispy brown bits you'll get. Cut the celery into 2–3 cm pieces, chop up the onion, and mince the garlic.

If you're using raw meat (like bacon, sausage or mince), cook it first in the skillet over medium heat, removing the meat when done and leaving the rendered fat in the pan. When the meat is cool enough to handle, cut, chop or crumble the meat into bite-sized chunks. If not, skip to the next step.

Over medium heat, heat some oil to the skillet and throw in the potatoes. Season well with salt and pepper. Leave the potatoes undisturbed for a few minutes in the pan (no stirring or shaking!) – they should start browning up.

After a few minutes, use the spatula to scrape and stir the potatoes, then leave them again for a couple of minutes to continue browning. If they are still very hard, add a little bit of water or stock to the pan, reduce the heat to low, and cover the pan so the potatoes can steam a bit. If they're already starting to soften up, you can skip this bit.

When the potatoes start to soften a bit, turn the heat back up to medium-high and add the carrots, onions, celery, and garlic, continuing the process of letting things cook undisturbed for a couple minutes, then scraping the brown bits off the bottom of the pan with the spatula and stirring everything up. If you are using pre-cooked (leftover) meat you can add it now.

Continue cooking, scraping the bottom of the pan and stirring until the potatoes and veggies are softened up to taste, well cooked, and the mixture is well browned. If you had cooked meat at the beginning and set it aside, you can add it now.

Taste the hash and season with salt and pepper as necessary. Serve immediately with a fried egg or two on top (for a super Sunday brekkie) or with a simple salad on the side for a quick and tasty weekday dinner.

Wild Mushroom and Herb Arancini

Alison Frith, artizian.co.uk

Alison says: "This recipe epitomises the very words 'use of leftovers', with all the ingredients coming from earlier meals, freeing up much needed time in a busy week. I secretly overproduce the risotto so that we can have arancini the next day for a light lunch with a few leaves and a 'tomato end' and herb salsa".

Serves 4

- 1 handful of dried wild mushrooms
- 1 white onion, peeled and sliced
- 3 tablespoons golden British rapeseed oil, plus some for drizzling
- 180g risotto rice
- 930ml vegetable stock
- 80ml white wine
- 3 frozen herb oil cubes
- 2–3 slices of bread ends, blitzed into crumbs

Start by soaking the dried wild mushrooms (a store cupboard favourite) in hot water to soften; this will provide you with a rich earthy liquor for the risotto rice to absorb.

Fry the onion in 3 tablespoons of oil, add the risotto rice and give it a few turns in the pan to coat. Strain in the mushroom liquor and add the vegetable stock and wine a bit at a time, stirring until absorbed and the rice is cooked.

Thinly slice the soaked wild mushrooms and add to the rice, followed by 2 or 3 herb oil cubes.

Chill the leftovers, then make 4 golf ball-sized arancini. You can use the flour and egg method of getting the breadcrumbs to stick to the arancini, but I prefer to let the natural stickiness of the risotto do the work for me!

Add a drizzle of rapeseed oil to an ovenproof frying pan, heat until very hot, then add your arancini, (but never shake the pan as it will break them up). Turn slowly so you get a nice golden colour. Transfer your pan to the oven for 10 minutes at 190°C/375°F/gas 5 or until piping hot in the middle.

Serve with a homemade tomato ends salsa and a few seasonal leaves; baby kale and pea shoots are my favourite. Enjoy!

Tip: I always try to keep any leftover loaf ends in the freezer, so for this recipe you just need two slices, defrosted and blitzed down into breadcrumbs.

Tomato Ends Salsa

Alison Frith, artizian.co.uk

Alison says: "Whenever I have an abundance of fresh garden herbs, I make frozen herb oil cubes. I whiz the herbs down with a touch of water or rapeseed oil, then freeze them in ice-cube trays, ready to pop into any dish".

Serves 4 as a side dish

- 20 saved tomato ends, roughly chopped
- 2 frozen herb oil cubes

Gather your tomato ends into a bowl and allow your herb oil cubes to melt slowly over them.

Bubble and Squeak

This is a Boxing Day favourite. It's fab served with an array of sliced cold meats, pickles and chutneys. It is also a great accompaniment to cooked breakfast.

- leftover cooked veg
- 1 tablespoon of oil

Mash up your leftover cooked veg in a food processor or with a hand blender. Heat the oil in a frying pan and add all the veg. Cook for 20 minutes, occasionally unsticking it from the pan and flipping halfway. For larger quantities, this will take a little longer and require a bit more turning.

Cornish Pasty

Another great way to use up leftover meat and veg. If you don't have enough leftover veg, swap in cooked potato or carrot, cut into cubes.

Makes 4 pasties

- shortcrust pastry (see recipe on page 116)
- leftover cooked meat, cut into small cubes
- leftover cooked veg

Roll out your pastry into a square, then quarter into 4 equal squares. Without cutting through, use your knife to gently mark diagonally across each square to make 2 triangles. Fill one triangle of each quarter with the cubed meat and veg leaving a generous border, then fold over and press down, crimping the edges together. Bake in the oven for 30 minutes at 200°C/400°F/gas 6, or until golden and piping hot, turning halfway.

Homity Pie

by Emma Marsh, Love Food Hate Waste

Emma says: "A traditional West Country open pie that's cheap, filling and quick to make. It's best eaten warm rather than hot, and it's really good cold so ideal for picnics or lunchboxes. It's also extremely versatile as you can add all sorts of ingredients. You can also make individual pies if you prefer."

Makes one x 20cm pie

- 150g flour (plain or gluten-free)
- 75ml sunflower oil (or vegetable oil), plus a dash for frying
- 250g cooked root vegetables, such as potatoes, parsnips and carrots
- 2 onions or leeks, chopped (150g)
- 2 unpeeled apples, chopped (200g)
- 3 rashers of bacon, shredded (100g)
- 75ml milk, cream, or plain yoghurt
- 100g cheese, grated
- 1 egg

Mix the flour, oil, 50ml of cold water and a pinch of salt into a dough. Cover and refrigerate for 15 minutes, then sprinkle with flour and roll out to ½cm thick, to line a lightly oiled 20cm x 4cm deep metal tin.

Meanwhile, add a dash of oil to a pan, add the bacon and onions, and stir regularly until the onions start to brown. Add the apples and potatoes and cook for a further 3 to 4 minutes, stirring regularly.

Now add the milk, ¾ of the cheese and a little salt and pepper, stir for 1 minute, then mix in the egg and put the mixture into the pastry case.

Top with the rest of the grated cheese and bake for 20 to 25 minutes at 180°C/350°F/gas 4 until golden brown.

Chef's tip from Lyndon
Preheat the oven and use a metal pie tin to make sure you get a crisp pastry base. If you use wholemeal flour for your pastry, add an extra dash of water.

Use up
Boiled, roast or baked potatoes. Other cooked vegetables like broccoli, cauliflower, green beans or squash. Or cooked chicken.

Variations
Use any cheese including blue or goat's cheese. Use pears instead of apples; add walnuts. Try smoked bacon or ham, chorizo or smoked haddock.

Extra flavour
Add herbs such as basil, parsley, oregano, chives or tarragon. Add a teaspoon of Dijon mustard or a teaspoon of curry paste. Or add crushed garlic.

Freezer advice
For best results, cool down quickly (ideally within an hour), divide into portions, place in an airtight container, label and pop in the freezer. Defrost in the fridge, ideally overnight, and use within 24 hours after defrosting. Reheat in the microwave or covered in foil in the oven, heating thoroughly until piping hot.

Vegetarian and vegan options
Use mushrooms or smoked tofu instead of bacon. Or use a vegan soya-based cream cheese instead of egg and milk.

Allergy advice
Can be made with gluten free flour, lactose free cheese and soya milk.

LUCKY PEEL

Case study – Luck Peel www.luckypeel.com

Globally over 60m tonnes of oranges are produced each year, with estimates suggesting that over a third of this is being thrown away as peel after juicing. 'Lucky Peel' are looking to change all that.

The London-based enterprise was founded by David and Gerard, two friends passionate about reducing the waste that comes with good food.

Starting with orange peel, their goal is to make the world fall in love with peel as an ingredient.

They work with juice bars in the heart of London to divert orange peel before it becomes waste, turning it into premium food and drink products. Their two best sellers are candied peel covered in chocolate and their 'Orangecello' liqueur (a delicious twist on traditional limoncello), both of which can be found at local markets and in a growing number of delis and shops across London.

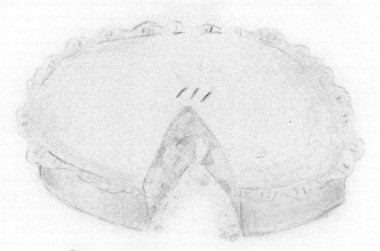

Better use of
the bits

Jam

by Jareth Mills, The Roebuck

Jareth says: "Any end of season, overly ripe fruit is best for jams and this gives you time to save all your citrus pips throughout a long summer of lemonade making (or gin drinking!) and keep them in a dry spot, a window sill is good. When you are ready and have a good large handful, tie them all together in a muslin bag, which of course can be washed and reused."

- a batch of summer fruits, a mixture or one of a kind is fine, washed and prepared
- a bag of pips for pectin
- sugar, one-third the weight of your fruits*
- any spices you desire

Put your fruit and pip bag into a large cooking pot – the mixture can almost triple in volume. Put on a low heat to help release the water from the fruit, but be careful not to catch it on the bottom of the pan at the start and the end by regularly folding in a figure of eight motion.

Once your mix is on, put a saucer in the freezer, this is for the set test when you think the jam may be ready. Turn the heat up when your fruit are positively swimming in their juices and reduce until it starts to thicken.

Add your sugar. At first, once the jam has started to boil it will look quite frothy, this is ok but you can skim it off if you like. This foaming will stop as the jam gets closer to setting point.

When you think the jam is ready (105°C), be mighty careful and squeeze any liquid from your bag of pips and stir the liquid into the jam, drop a dollop of jam on your frozen saucer and return it to the freezer for 15 minutes.When you push your finger through the cold saucer dollop, the skin should wrinkle and it should hold its shape quite well. If not, simmer further and repeat until it does.

Lesser set jams are totally fine and delicious but for an actual preserve that will last, there must be a high enough percentage of sugar and low amount of water activity, this is why the temperature can be important.

When finished, decant carefully into sterilised containers that can be made airtight and store, in theory, indefinitely.

Personally, I like chunky jams so I'm most likely to leave berries and things whole, just removing the stalks. And remember to check for grubs in blackberries!

*A lot of jam recipes will state a 1:1 ratio of fruit to sugar but not according to Marguerite Patten and one particularly stern WI matron she met whilst working for the ministry of food during WW2, and who should know better than the WI!

Apple Membrillo for Cheese

by Jareth Mills, The Roebuck

Jareth says: "Membrillo is the Spanish word for quince, the traditional ingredient for this sweet cheese accompaniment. During the autumn we make a lot of apple crumble and I couldn't bear to see all that trim go in the waste any longer, so this recipe came from a hunch that it would work and a hope it would be nice! It was and we manage to make enough in autumn and winter to last us the year."

- any amount of apple peel and cores (the more the better!)
- sugar

Cover the apple trimmings with cold water in a pan and bring to the boil. Leave to cook until all structure of the flesh has gone. Your kitchen will smell so wonderfully of apples! Drain, keeping 1 litre of the boiling liquor to help with lubrication.

Pass the pulp through ever increasingly fine sieves and 'chinois' (a conical sieve), adding the liquor as you go to aid the process. When you've got your required purée, weigh and subtract the weight of the water you added. Divide this number by three and this is the weight of sugar you need to add.

Put the mix back into a pan and carefully reduce to a thick paste. Be extra careful as the mix spits like molten lava from a volcano so it's probably best to cook it in a high-sided pan. It will stick and darken but this is caramelisation at work and as long as it doesn't blacken and you keep folding it back through the mix, it's all flavour! When it is thick enough to hold its shape for a few seconds remove from the heat and spoon into jars or moulds (if you want to be able to turn out the set membrillo remember to line your mould with a double layer of cling film.).

Candied Citrus Peel

The hardest thing about making your own candied peel is to save enough peel to make it worthwhile spending the 10 minutes it takes to prepare. I never think it is worth it for just a couple of peels, so I have experimented with the best way to keep the peel. I now keep it in the freezer until I have a bagful.

- any quantity of citrus peel, such as oranges, lemons, limes, tangerines, diced
- sugar

In a saucepan, cover the peel with water and bring to the boil. Turn down the heat and simmer for 5 minutes, drain and toss out onto a baking tray, then sprinkle with just enough sugar to coat the peel. Bake in the oven on the lowest setting (around 80°C/175°F/gas 1) for about 30 minutes. Cool, then store in an airtight jar.

Vegetable Peel Stock

Vegetable peel stock is a great base for low calorie meals and vegan or vegetarian dishes. Gather up all your vegetable peel throughout the week into a tub in the fridge; tops and ends, the shavings of browned lettuce, the outer edges of your broccoli and cauliflower stalks. I have even made vegetable stock with just onion skins when that's all I've had to hand. You can get a rich flavour and some deep colours, making a perfect base for soup or risotto, or to add to casseroles or gravy. If I don't use up my collection of bits at the weekend I might pop it into the freezer for the next time I'm making a big batch of stock or soup. If I forget sometimes, which certainly has been known, I just pop it in the compost, wash my tub and start my collection anew.

• any amount of vegetable skins, peels, and end bits

Put all your ingredients into a large saucepan with enough water to cover them. Bring to the boil, then turn down the heat and simmer gently for about 25 minutes. Strain and cool, then keep in a container in the fridge for a few days, or freeze.

Fish Stock

Fish stock is great for making the most of your filets of fish. Even if you ask your fishmonger to fillet the fish for you, you can ask to take all the leftover bits with you. You can pop them in the freezer until you have time to cook up your fish stock: this is great for fishy risottos, fish soup or chowder.

- fish heads, tails and bones
- a handful of mixed herbs
- any vegetable peelings, such as onion skins or leek ends, roughly chopped

Put all your ingredients into a large saucepan with enough water to cover them. Bring to the boil, then turn down the heat and simmer gently for about 25 minutes. Strain and cool, then keep in a container in the fridge for a few days, or freeze.

Chicken Stock

by Thomasina Miers, author of The Home Cook (Faber)

Thomasina says: "Forget any cheffy connotations, making stock is easy and a fine example of getting something for almost nothing. Re-use the bones from your roast, cover them with water and let them do all the work. If you don't have the energy to deal with making stock straight after a filling roast dinner, then you can leave it until the next day to strain, cool and store it. I use clean plastic milk cartons to store my stock in the fridge or freezer.

"Bear in mind the source of your stock; high-quality meat from farms or good butchers means strong bones that give beautifully jellied, highly nutritious stock."

- 1 chicken carcass with all the leftover gunk (skin, fat, jelly etc.)
- 1 large onion, cut into chunks
- 2 carrots, cut into chunks
- 2 celery sticks, cut into chunks
- 1 teaspoon whole peppercorns
- few sprigs of parsley or thyme
- 2 bay leaves, preferably (but not necessarily) fresh
- 2 unpeeled garlic cloves (optional)

Probably the most useful of all the different kinds, a chicken stock will add flavour to sauces, risottos, stews and soups and can transform store cupboard noodles into exotic bowls of Asian pho. The most obvious way to make a chicken stock is by using the bones and leftovers from a roast, but if you are making a stock from a fresh, raw chicken, begin by cooking the chicken in a hot oven for 20 minutes to get some caramelisation and depth of flavour. If you are using a leftover carcass, adding the raw neck, or gizzard, and some giblets will improve the taste; they usually come free with the bird from a butcher or farmers market.

Put all the ingredients into a pan just large enough to fit them and cover with water. Bring to the boil, then reduce the heat and simmer gently for 2–3 hours. Top up the stock with hot water as it evaporates so that the ingredients are always covered, but never boil vigorously or the stock will taste bitter. Strain and cool, then chill in the fridge. When cold, spoon off any fat that has collected on the surface.

To freeze the stock, pour into clean plastic water bottles or milk containers and mark the contents and date on them with a freezer pen (it keeps happily for 6 months). Alternatively reduce the stock right down after you have strained it to produce a highly concentrated essence. You can then freeze this in ice-cube trays; perfect if a recipe calls for only a small amount of stock.

Kitchen Note:
Never add salt to stock in case you need to reduce it later; the salt levels can become too concentrated the more it is reduced.

Chard Stem and Black-eyed Bean Salad

My great friend, Ülfet, gave me this lovely way of making chard stems into something wonderful rather than the discard they often are. Ülfet really knows how to make the best of food and bring out flavour in everything. This dish is simple and cheap to make, and delicious.

Serves 4 as a side dish

- chard stems
- 1 can black-eyed beans
- olive oil
- 1 lemon

Steam the chard stems for about 15 to 20 minutes until tender but with a slight resistance when you put a fork in. Leave to cool.

Drain the black-eyed beans, setting aside the liquid for use in soup or stock. Drizzle the beans with olive oil and lemon juice and season with sea salt. It makes a pretty salad, delicious and full of goodness.

Carrot Top Pesto

Carrot tops are such a beautiful vibrant green it seems such a shame to waste them, yet that's what so many people do. Here's how to make your own homemade carrot top pesto, for when you grow your own carrots or for the rare occasions you buy them with their tops on.

- carrot tops, washed and finely chopped
- Parmesan cheese, grated
- handful of pine nuts
- 1 large or 2 small cloves of garlic (smoked garlic is nice), peeled and finely chopped
- olive oil

Push your chopped carrot tops down into a sterilised glass jar. Take a look at the jam recipes for how to sterilise your jars. Add the Parmesan, pine nuts and chopped garlic, then put the lid on and give it a shake to mix it up a bit.

Open the jar and pour in some olive oil. Put the lid back on and give it a good shake again. You may need to stir it up at this point. Once it's well mixed, add a bit more oil to make sure it's all covered.

Seal the jar and refrigerate. It will keep for several weeks in the fridge. Just like shop-bought pesto, keep topping up with olive oil to cover so it keeps for longer.

Radish Pesto

by Sally-Jayne Wright, sally-jaynewright.co.uk

Sally says: "The hotter the radishes, the better your pesto will taste. I've eaten this with wholemeal penne, on cauliflower salad as a dressing and spread on toast with fresh tomatoes. It keeps very well, covered with oil, in a recycled, plastic humus carton with a tight-fitting lid."

- leaves from a bunch of radishes (2 generous handfuls), stems removed
- 30g pecorino or Parmesan cheese, finely grated
- 30g ground almonds
- 3 tablespoons extra virgin olive oil
- 1 fat clove of garlic, peeled and germ (the green bit in the middle) removed
- a small strip of lemon peel, pith removed or lemon juice, to taste

Wash and dry the radish leaves thoroughly, discarding any that are mushy or yellow. Pulse all the ingredients in the bowl of a small blender, pushing down the contents from time to time and adding more oil, if necessary, to form a thick green paste.

Broccoli Stalk Gravy

by Dean Pearce, @FoodRecycleDean

Dean says: "I always keep broccoli stalks. When I'm making the Sunday roast, I use the broccoli stalks in my gravy as a thickener. For a chicken gravy, I finely chop the stalks, fry them in butter with two garlic bulbs and one onion until all the ingredients are soft, but not burnt. I add a glass of wine (then usually pour a second glass for tasting purposes!) and simmer off the alcohol.

"I add the defrosted stock from the bones of a previous chicken roast, the water from the boiled potatoes and any veg I might have parboiled (such as cauliflower), with any juice from the meat currently in the oven. I'll let that simmer for 10 to 15 minutes so that everything is soft.

"I add a few sprigs of fresh tarragon (I always put any excess herbs in the freezer - they keep very well for months), thyme, a couple of bay leaves, a teaspoon of marmite and a dash of soy sauce. I then blitz it with the hand-blender until it's perfectly smooth and leave to simmer until the dinner is ready, ensuring that I add any last bits from the roasting tin and blend those in too for extra flavour. Finally I'll season to taste.

"I've learnt from experience that seasoning is best left to the last minute, especially when you're allowing something to simmer and reduce. Sometimes I add a bit of cream and blend that in too or an extra stock cube if the flavour doesn't have enough depth."

Use-it-up Salad Dressing

One of my zero waste specials

I always like to make sure I make the most of everything. I remember hearing people talk about Coleman's mustard, saying that Mr Coleman made his money not from the mustard people ate, but what they left on the side of their plate. Not in my house. We even use what we can't get out of the jar with a knife, as a base for salad dressing.

Take a jar of mustard that's pretty much finished. Add some vinegar, such as cider vinegar, wine vinegar or I've even used the vinegar from a jar of pickles. Pour in some olive oil, add in a generous twist or ten of black pepper and put the lid on tight. Shake it all about to get every last bit of mustard from the side of the jar and there you have it: delicious, zero-waste salad dressing.

Potato Skins with Cheese and Bacon

After years of ordering this in restaurants, we started to make mash potato in a way that we could use the skins for this yummy starter. You can keep the potato skins in the fridge for a few days or you can freeze them, for when you want to make your potato skin starter.

Allow 2 or 3 half skins per person

- bacon
- Cheddar or red Leicester or mozzarella, grated
- potato skins from baked potatoes

Cook your bacon, then chop it into small pieces. Mix the bacon pieces with your grated cheese and fill your potato skins. Warm them in the oven or place them under the grill until the cheese melts. Simple and delicious.

Potato Skins with Cream Cheese and Chives

A vegetarian version of the cheese and bacon skins

Allow 2 or 3 half skins per person

- cream cheese
- chopped chives
- chopped spring onions

Mix the cream cheese with the chopped chives and spring onion. Warm your potato skins in the oven or microwave and then fill with the cream cheese mix. Serve immediately so the skins are still warm but the filling cold. The combination works well.

Easy Mashed Potato

- baked potatoes (use one large baked potato per person)
- butter
- milk

Halve your baked potatoes and scoop out the middle, leaving the skins intact for another meal. Add some butter and milk and mash with a fork or potato masher, season to taste and there you have your mashed potato.

Faggots

by Cara Harrison, lowcostliving.co.uk

Cara says: "Faggots are a great way to get more organ meats into your diet. A lot of people aren't keen on the taste of liver, heart, and other offal, but find faggots to be flavourful and not as strong tasting. Don't chuck away any leftover stock from cooking them. This can be added to the gravy along with some fried onions.

"This faggots recipe is a firm family favourite, especially comforting on a cold winter's day. I have also made this in the slow cooker and find they take 4 to 5 hours on high to be perfectly cooked. Delicious served with onion gravy, mashed potatoes and peas or buttered greens."

Serves 4 to 6

- 450g pig's liver, trimmed and roughly chopped
- 350g belly pork, chopped
- 2 medium onions, peeled and roughly chopped
- 120g breadcrumbs
- 1 egg, beaten
- 1 teaspoon salt
- ½ teaspoon black pepper
- 1 teaspoon dried mixed herbs
- 150ml beef stock

Preheat the oven to 180°C/350°F/gas 4.

Put the liver, pork and onions in a food processor and process until finely chopped. If you don't have a food processor, you'll need to finely chop by hand or use a grater where possible. Tip into a large mixing bowl and stir in the breadcrumbs, egg, salt, pepper and mixed herbs until fully combined.

With wet hands, shape the mixture into 12 patties and lay them in an ovenproof dish. Pour in the stock. Use a buttered sheet of foil to cover the dish (buttered-side down).

Crimp the edges of the foil around the dish to seal them. Cook in the oven for about 45 minutes until the faggots are cooked (the juices should run clear when they are pierced with a knife).

Remove the foil, then turn up the temperature on the oven to 200°C/400°F/gas 6 and return the faggots to the oven and cook for a further 10 minutes until lightly browned.

Sage and Onion Stuffing

We have lots of fresh sage in our garden and always have onions in stock.
Stuffing is simple to make and is a good way of using up bits and pieces.

Serves 4 to 6

- 1 onion finely chopped
- 1 tablespoon of olive oil, butter or bacon fat
- bread or breadcrumbs – the quantity can vary according to what you have available
- sage, a handful roughly chopped
- bits of apple core and peel minus the pips (optional)
- any bits of meat, sausages, bacon, paté that need using up (optional)
- 1 egg to bind the mixture (or 2 if you have a lot of breadcrumbs)

Fry the onion lightly. Whiz the bread in a food processor to make breadcrumbs. Add the chopped sage, salt and pepper, and your bits of apple and meat if using and whiz a bit more. Beat your egg and add to the mixture, giving it a good stir up then mix in the fried onion. Transfer it to an oven-proof dish and press it down. Bake in the oven for about 45 minutes to an hour.
You can also cook it inside a roast chicken.

Sausage Roll

by Karen Burns-Booth, lavenderandlovage.com

Karen says: "This recipe is from One-Pot Meals – Ministry of Food Leaflet Number 35. The sausage roll can be steamed in two old baked beans tins... hence the recipe name sausage roll I suspect!"

Serves 4

- 225g sausagemeat
- 2 tablespoons of finely chopped onion or leek
- 1 tablespoon of chopped pickled veg or chutney
- 85g breadcrumbs
- a pinch of mixed herbs
- a pinch of pepper
- 1½ teaspoons salt
- 2 tablespoons of stock or milk

Mix all the ingredients together thoroughly. Turn into a greased tin and steam for 1½ to 2 hours.

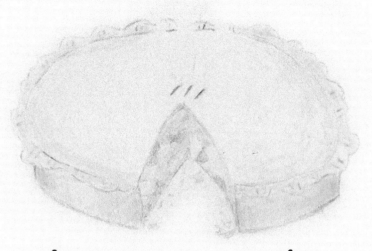

Use it up snacks and light lunches

Olio Guac

by Saascha Celestial-One, Co-founder of OLIO, the food sharing app,
OLIOex.com

Saascha says: "The word 'OLIO' means 'a miscellaneous collection of things', and this principle is applied to just about anything I cook in the kitchen (with the exception perhaps of a Victoria sponge or other cake, requiring an element of precision). I like to make Guacamole in the OLIO fashion – crunchy, creamy, delicious, and totally random. Not only is it healthier and more filling, it's a great way to use up spare veg knocking around the kitchen."

Serves 4 as a starter

- 2 medium or 1 large, ripe avocado, mashed (did you know you can put an avocado that's just achieved perfect ripeness to the touch in the fridge, where it will last for many more days than if left out in the open?)
- equal quantity to the avocado of very finely diced chopped vegetables – whatever needs eating, be it carrots, celery, radishes, courgettes, sugar snap peas, broccoli stem … be creative!
- 1 small red or white onion, finely diced
- 1 medium tomato, chopped (or a handful of quartered cherry tomatoes)
- handful of coriander or parsley, shredded or finely chopped
- ½ juice of a fresh lime (or lemon or orange, depending on what you have going)
- 1 jalapeno, diced (leave the seeds in if you like it hot)
- $1/_8$ teaspoon garlic powder or 1 garlic clove, finely chopped
- pumpkin or sunflower seeds (optional)

Mix all ingredients together, salt to taste, and sprinkle with pumpkin or sunflower seeds. Serve with corn tortilla or pita chips as an appetiser, or spread onto toasted bread for a delicious sandwich base. And, if you're eyes are bigger than your stomach and you have Guacamole going spare, why not offer it on OLIO for a lovely neighbour to collect?

Vegetable Crisps

by Jenny Costa, Rubies in the Rubble

Jenny says: "This is a super simple recipe and is a fantastic way to make the most of your veg. Whether you're making vegetable soup or mashed potato, think twice before binning the peel. Instead, pop them in the oven to make delicious crisps – perfect as a side dish or to accompany the Olio Guac."

Preheat the oven to 200°C/ 400°F/gas 6. Put the peel in a large baking tray and drizzle with olive oil and seasoning: we recommend salt, pepper, cumin and a dusting of chilli powder for all you who like to live on the veg. Toss the tray to ensure an even spread of the seasoning. Roast for 15 to 20 minutes. Stir halfway through roasting, and remove them once they're done to your liking. Once the peels are cool enough to eat, devour without delay! Why not use our chutneys as a dipping sauce? Or mix some yoghurt into London Piccalilli for a delicious Tzatziki style dip.

Spanish Omelette

Whenever I make omelette I always hear the sound of my friend Antoine's voice decreeing that you should always 'lift' an omelette with a little water or milk. So I always have.

Serves 2

· 4 eggs (or 6 if you are really hungry and haven't got much filling)
· salt and pepper
· a drop of water or milk
· for the 'filling' you can throw in whatever you have to use up in the fridge, like tomatoes, peppers, grated cheese, ham, chorizo, roast or boiled potatoes, herbs

Beat the eggs and add a drop of water or milk and mix it in. Season with a pinch of salt and some black pepper. Heat a flat-bottomed frying pan. Then pour in the egg mixture. When the egg is nearly cooked (i.e. mostly solid rather than runny) add your filling. Allow to heat through and gently fold half of the omelette over the other half. We love omelette served with a herb salad picked from the garden in the summer or baked beans in the winter.

Paneer

from Sara Green, Derby Food Assembly

Sara says: "Milk is something that feels horrible to waste, but if you do have some milk that's just starting to go sour then a really easy way to use it is to make paneer, perfect to add to a curry later on. It is a mild milky cheese which absorbs other flavours really well, which is why it's a staple of Indian cooking. It is best to use whole milk for this recipe."

· Milk
· Lemon juice

You will need a muslin or cheese cloth

Put milk in a pan and bring to the boil, then turn down the heat and add a good amount of lemon juice to cause the milk to curdle.

Leave the milk to cool for 10 minutes before pouring into a sieve lined with a muslin or cheese cloth. Rinse with cold water and then squeeze the cloth to remove any extra liquid (whey). Weight down with something heavy, such as a heavy saucepan, to squeeze more liquid out.

Leave in the fridge to set, and slice up to cook later.

Watermelon 'Fois Gras'

by Gill Watson, Chef and Food Activist

Gill says: "Watermelon is something I have many a time picked up at the end of the day from markets. When we rescue it, we have to extend its life in order to then distribute it to families who might not otherwise get to eat enough fresh fruit. I might juice it, or make sorbet, but here is an interesting way to use up rescued watermelons."

Use either watermelon or piel de sapo, sliced into seedless rectangles, sprinkled lightly with salt and then placed in a resealable food bag to be kept in the fridge overnight.

Drain off the excess juice the next day, dry on kitchen paper and they you're ready to fry it. Brown a little butter in a frying pan and fry the slices until coloured on each side.

Serve with duck, tuna, or as part of an unusual vegan feast.

Don't forget to save the rind for making little watermelon houses for gerbils!

Cheesy toasties

by Carole Bamford, owner of Daylesford Organic: www.daylesford.com and The Wild Rabbit: www.thewildrabbit.co.uk

Carole says: "My family adore cheese. This is a quick, simple, no frills way of getting rid of leftover bits from the larder. It is fabulous on a Sunday evening when you have eaten a good lunch, but just need a little something to tide you over while you watch 'Call the Midwife'."

Take leftover pieces of cheese and grate. Lightly toast a tasty slice of bread, I adore Daylesford Organics Spelt Sourdough. Butter sparingly, top with assorted types of grated cheese. Place under the grill until bubbly and moulten.

Cut into fingers or squares, flop into a comfy chair with the dog at your feet and enjoy each and every mouthful. The perfect way to end a wonderful weekend!

Mango, Ginger and Cardamom Cookies

by Pamela Higgins, spamellab.com

Pamela says: " This is a super easy and deliciously spiced cookie recipe using the Apple and Mango 'Snact' fruit jerky. The ginger and cardamom work wonderfully with coconut to create these tasty snacks when your sweet tooth is calling out to you!

Makes 9 to 12 cookies

- 1 cup rolled oats
- ½ cup desiccated coconut
- 2 tablespoons coconut flour
- ½ teaspoon ground cardamom
- ½ teaspoon ground ginger
- 2 tablespoons coconut sugar
- 3 tablespoons coconut oil
- 2 tablespoons almond butter
- 1 packet Snact Apple & Mango Fruit Jerky
- 3 tablespoons maple syrup or natural fruit syrup
- extra dried mango and coconut chips to decorate

Preheat the oven to 180°C/350°F/gas 4 and grease and line a baking tray.

Mix together the oats, desiccated coconut, coconut flour, cardamom and ginger in a bowl. Chop the fruit jerky into very small pieces and stir into the dry ingredients.

Melt the coconut oil, almond butter and syrup in a small pan, then remove from the heat.

Pour into the dry ingredients and mix well to combine and it sticks together a little. Divide into about 9–12 cookies and press down onto the tray.

Bake for about 10 minutes until golden, then leave to cool so they firm up a bit more. Sprinkle over the coconut chips, decorate with a slice of dried mango and drizzle with a little more syrup.

Blueberry, Apple and Banana Energy Bars

by Pamela Higgins, spamellab.com

Pamela says: "This one uses Snact Apple, Blueberry & Banana jerky, making an ideal breakfast on-the-go or pre/post workout boost."

Makes 9 to 12 bars

- 2 cups rolled oats
- 2 tablespoons coconut or almond flour
- 3 tablespoons chia seeds
- 4 tablespoons flaked almonds (or use pumpkin seeds)
- 1 teaspoon cinnamon
- 1 x packet Snact Apple, Blueberry & Banana Fruit Jerky
- 2 tablespoons coconut oil
- 3 tablespoons nut butter (almond, cashew or peanut)
- 4 tablespoons maple syrup
- 1 large banana, mashed, 1 small apple, grated
- 1 teaspoon vanilla extract
- ½ cup fresh blueberries

Preheat the oven to 180°C/350°F/gas 4 and grease and line a rectangular baking tray.

Mix together the oats, chia seeds, almonds (or seeds) and cinnamon in a large bowl. Using clean kitchen scissors, snip the fruit jerky pieces into little pieces and mix into the dry ingredients.

Gently melt the coconut oil, nut butter and maple syrup in a small pan on the hob. Set aside and leave to cool for about 5 minutes.

Pour this into the dry ingredients along with the mashed banana, grated apple and vanilla, stirring well to combine. Leave to stand for 5 minutes to let the chia seeds thicken the mixture.

Now stir in the blueberries and mix in to distribute. Spoon the mixture into your tin and smooth out evenly. Bake for 15–20 minutes, until golden and firm. Leave to cool completely in the tin, then cut into 9–12 bars and remove. Enjoy!

Crispy Fried Salt and Pepper Banana Skins

by Lorna Hall, eatmyyythoughts.com

Lorna says: "If you're wondering if banana skins are edible, the answer is: yes, they are! Some people argue against eating banana skins, solely because monkeys don't eat them. But monkeys can't cook. When you think about it, monkeys don't eat orange peels either, but I don't think that's any reason for people to give up eating marmalade.

"Banana peels are used to make things like curries and chutneys in other parts of the world; they're just not a popular ingredient in the West. But they're actually really tasty! Over-ripe peels can be boiled with vanilla and cardamom to make a delicious banana tea. But these crispy peels are also really, really good. Banana skins have a savoury flavour. This complements sweeter vegetables like sweet potatoes but also adds depth of flavour to other vegetable dishes."

Serves 2

- 1 tablespoon garlic oil
- 3 banana skins, thoroughly washed and cut into thin strips, around 7cms long.
- 2 spring onions, sliced
- 2 red chillies, sliced
- salt and pepper

Heat a medium-sized frying pan on high heat. Add the garlic oil. Add generous amounts of salt and pepper to a bowl and toss the banana skins in the seasoning. Add the seasoned skins to the frying pan and allow them to crisp up in the hot oil. This usually takes around 10 to 15 minutes.

When the skins are almost crispy, add the spring onions and red chillies and continue to fry for a further 5 minutes. Serve as a topping on mashed sweet potato or alongside a curry, with some fresh coriander.

Spinach Quiche

When our perpetual spinach (which is actually chard) is in full flow, it seems to grow again as soon as your back is turned after picking. So using up my spinach feels like food for free.

Makes 1 x 24cm quiche

For the pastry
· 150g plain flour
· 75g butter
· 60–80g water

For the filling
· 4 eggs, beaten
· a dash of milk
· salt and pepper
· grated cheddar
· spinach
· you could also add in any bacon, feta cheese, or sweetcorn if you have any

First make up your pastry following the recipe for Chicken and Leek Pie. Use the trimmings to make Parmesan Bites (page 186).

Roll out your pastry and line your quiche dish, allowing it to overlap the sides of the dish. Using a knife cut off the spare pastry from round the outside edge of the dish. Use baking parchment or a reusable silicone cake dish liner to cover the pastry on the bottom of the dish and fill with baking beans. Blind bake the pastry case for 20 minutes at 200°C/400°F/gas 6.

Fill the part cooked pastry cake with the spinach and crumble in the feta cheese. Add the bacon and sweetcorn if using.

Beat the eggs and add a dash of milk and season with salt and pepper. If you have both feta and bacon you can omit the salt. Pour the beaten egg over the filling of the quiche. Bake at 190°C/375°F/gas 5 for a further 30 minutes. The filling will be fairly solid to the touch when it is cooked.

Parmesan Bites

These are a great way to use up your pastry scraps.

Knead together your pastry scraps into a ball and press flat. Roll out and cut using a small biscuit cutter or use an egg cup. Pick up any remaining scraps, knead and roll out again. Press the last few scraps into shape to be your taster biscuit. Transfer your biscuits onto a baking sheet, and then sprinkle with black pepper and parmesan cheese.

Bake at 200°C/400°F/gas 6 for 12 to 15 minutes until golden.

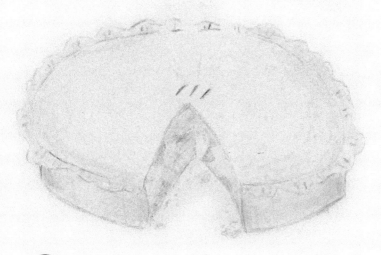

Soups and sauces

Nail Soup

by Jo Wright, simplybeingmum.com

Jo says: "Did you ever hear the story of 'Nail Soup', the traditional Swedish folk tale?

"The story starts with a tramp knocking at a little old lady's door in need of shelter, and ends with a cosy gathering around her wooden table, with them both enjoying a hearty soup made from little more than a bent nail.

"Of course, the soup contained more than one solitary nail. It also contained salt, vegetables and meat. The charm of the story is in the infinite potential to create something from seemingly nothing. To start with very little, just a nail, and by scouring the store cupboard (and one's imagination) a meal is conjured up from various ingredients.

"The analytical among us may not find the story that charming, a cynical viewpoint would be it's a tale about a con-artist who tricks a potentially vulnerable lady. But for this recipe we'll brush that aside and focus on the more positive aspects. Just a little bit of this and a little bit of that can make something so much more.

"I'm calling 'Nail Soup' a recipe in the broadest of terms, for the beauty of this is, there is no recipe to follow – just an example of how to think beyond a list of ingredients. By taking bits of this and bits of that, and by getting creative in the kitchen, you can use up food you already have. Ingredients that could otherwise lead to waste."

Serves 2

- 500ml boiling water or stock
- 1 onion, finely chopped
- herbs (I usually use mixed, dried herbs for ease)
- vegetables, cut into equal bitesize pieces

One thing you should not add to your soup is a nail. Nails (whether straight or bent) are best left in the realms of fairy tales and folklore!

Pre-heat the standard-sized slow-cooker following the manufacturer's guidelines.

Load the pot to approximately half its capacity with vegetables. Ensure root vegetables such as carrots and parsnips are in equal bitesize pieces and do the same with potato - placing such vegetables at the bottom of the pot as they take longer to cook and soften. Add the onion.

Add approx. 500ml of boiling hot vegetable stock or water. The cooker should be two-thirds full, with at least a 2.5cm gap at the top to the lid. If you need more fluid simply top up with boiling water.

Herbs and spices can be added. This is a particularly good idea when not using stock as it helps to enhance the flavour. Crushed garlic is also an option. When first experimenting stick to dried mixed-herbs, a little black pepper and a pinch of salt

Cook on high for 4 hours or 8 hours on low

Leave to cool a little and then carefully blend. This is easiest done in the pot using a hand blender.

Serve immediately, or alternatively refrigerate for up to 3 days or freeze and use within 1 month.

Variations:

Some combinations will work better than others. For example apple works well with parsnip and leeks work well with potato. The idea is to give all sorts of combinations a try. A mixed vegetable soup generally will also turn out pretty good, whether blended, or part blended (to part blend remove some of the soup from the pot prior to blending then add back in).

For those who like a denser or more filling soup, simply add some cooked and drained lentils toward the end of the cooking time, before blending. Lentils are great for bulking up a meal and are something I always keep in my store cupboard. Or you could try a variation of minestrone soup, a broth with a mix of vegetables and also in some cases, pasta, rice and beans. By adding in these other ingredients you can easily transform a light meal into dinner, particularly by accompanying the meal with bread rolls.

If, like me, you enjoy getting the taste-buds tingling in the dishes you serve, then add a heaped dessert spoon of curry paste before blending to provide the desired kick. This works best with root vegetable or squash based soups.

I tend not to add meat, but you can. Please follow food safety guidelines for reheating the exact meat you are including. Ensure that it is cooked throughout and if serving up your soup at a later date, make sure it's reheated correctly to reduce the possibility of harmful bacteria.

Frugal Green Soup

by Rachelle Strauss, zerowasteweek.co.uk

Rachelle says: "This is a great recipe for using up all the odds and ends of vegetables, including things some people might normally throw away such as the green ends of leeks, broccoli stalks and the outer sprout leaves. As you might guess, these ingredients are rough as it depends what you have to use up at home. It's a bit of a 'good for you' soup as it's packed full of greens and ends up bright green when cooked."

Serves 2

- 1 tablespoon olive oil
- ends of leeks I've saved up during the week, roughly chopped
- 2 garlic cloves, smashed
- handful of sprouts (or outer leaves and stalks I've cut off during the week)
- broccoli stalks, sliced
- ½ bag kale
- 1 medium potato, diced (I've been known to chuck left over jacket potato skins in there too!)
- herbs of your choice (I usually use mixed, dried herbs for ease)
- Tamari sauce
- water or stock
- half a tin of chickpeas or some shredded chicken (optional to make it more filling)
- seasoning to taste

Soften the onion and garlic in the oil in a large pan.

Add the rest of the veggies except the kale and mix around for a minute or two in the hot oil.

Add the water or stock, tamari and herbs to taste. Add however much water or stock you want depending on your preference for a thick or thinner soup.

Bring to the boil, then simmer for around 12 minutes until the potato is cooked through.

Add the kale and warm through for another few minutes until it wilts then remove from heat.

Add any other ingredients to make the soup more filling such as chicken, chickpeas, lentils etc plus seasoning.

Blitz until desired consistency.

Broccoli and Blue Cheese Soup

My broccoli and blue cheese soup often doesn't have a single floret of broccoli in it, but you would never know. I use up the leaves and stem of cauliflower, and the stalk of broccoli and the rind of my blue cheese. The first time I made this soup, I was just making it for myself, so I really didn't worry too much about whether it tasted like broccoli and stilton soup, I just wanted it to taste nice. However, I had an unexpected visit from my cousins, and so we shared the soup. Naomi said it was the nicest broccoli and stilton soup she had ever had. I'm not sure if I've ever told her what was in it, but now she will know!

Serves 4

- 1 tablespoon oil
- 1 onion, peeled and chopped
- 1 leek, chopped including the leafy green part
- a couple of celery or lovage stalks and leaves, chopped
- 1 litre chicken or vegetable stock
- cauliflower leaves and stalk, chopped
- broccoli stem, chopped
- any cheese rind and old bits of cheese that need using up

Sweat the onion, leeks and celery in the oil. Add the stock and the cauliflower leaves and broccoli stalks. Bring to the boil and then turn down the heat, add in your cheese and allow to simmer for 25 to 30 minutes. Blitz with a hand blender, taste and season with salt and black pepper.

Cucumber Soup

from John and Val Harrison's www.allotment-garden.org website

This recipe was sent in to the website by Pat Arnell. It freezes well so it is a great way to prolong the life of your cucumbers.

Serves 2

- 800g cucumber
- 2 tablespoons virgin olive oil
- 4 spring onions
- 225g potatoes
- 500 to 750ml chicken or vegetable stock

Cut cucumbers in half lengthways; scoop out seeds and discard them; chop cucumber finely. Finely chop spring onions and finely chop potatoes. Heat oil in large pan and sauté spring onions and cucumber for a few minutes then add potatoes and stock. Bring to the boil and simmer for approx. 20 minutes until vegetables are tender. Adjust seasoning and serve.

Bean Broth, Made Good

by Malou Herkes, wonkyvegblog.com

Malou says: "Bean broth, bean juice, bean liquid. Whatever appetising name you like to call it (there aren't any), that murky liquid from a tin of butter beans or the cooking water from a tender chickpea, is liquid gold. Liquid gold! Especially, when saved for a rainy, bare-fridge kinda day.

"That day came. A jar of chickpea cooking liquid sat on the fridge shelf alongside a lone onion and an egg. The hummus had been eaten. So, I chopped the onion and fried it in oil, cos that's what you do when you want to cook something isn't it? In went the chickpea juice, a smidge of bouillon and a good splash of hot water.

"At this point, I found two wilted kale leaves so I chopped them and added them to the mix, and brought it all to the boil. Taste and season.

"I beat the egg and stirred it in, off the heat – the egg span into white ribbons, the soup thickened into a nice creamy-looking broth. It looked better already. Very tasty in fact.

"My mum swears by the power of a cracked egg; into hot broth, mashed potato, veggie juices. It adds flavour, substance and sustenance. Mark her words. Try cracking an egg into any sad-looking two-day-old soup or broth, and it'll revive it into something more satisfying. The Italians do a similar thing, too. Beat an egg with grated Parmesan, and pour it into boiling meat broth until you get little stracciatelle – literally meaning, shreds – of egg.

"Serve straight-up with a hunk of toasted bread, and – if you have it – a generous grating of mature cheese, or a sprinkling of fresh herb leaves, or a drizzle of olive oil. Bloomin' marvellous."

Leek and Lettuce Soup

My aunt, Rina, first introduced me to leek and lettuce soup. You can use up the entire leek and it is a good way to use up the outer leaves of your lettuce or the cut edge of an iceberg lettuce that has gone brown. We also use up the bags of warm salad that come with an Indian takeaway in this soup. The salad is of course only warm as it has travelled in a bag of hot dishes, so it often gets left as we tuck in to our takaway. This way, the limp salad doesn't go to waste.

Serves 2

* 1 tablespoon olive oil
* 1 onion
* 2 large or 3 small leeks, the entire leek, roots and leaves as well
* 500 to 750ml of chicken or vegetable stock
* letttuce, whatever, you would no longer eat as salad - any amount

Chop off the leek root and the leefy green part, then chop the main white part and bottom section of the green part of the leek into rounds and wash thoroughly to remove any soil. Heat the olive oil in a large pan and sweat the onion and leek rounds.

While that is going on, wash the leek roots very throughly to remove all the soil and chop them up, then add to the onion and leek already in the pan and swish around for a couple of minutes. Add the chicken stock and bring to the boil.

Wash the green leafy part of the leek and drain then chop it up roughly and add to the pan. Chop up your lettuce and add it. Once it has boiled for a couple of minutes, turn down the heat and allow it to simmer for about 25 to 30 minutes. Blitz with a hand blender, taste and season with salt and black pepper.

Chinese Style Chicken and Sweetcorn Soup

by Cara Harrison, www.lowcostliving.co.uk

Cara says: "I love Chinese chicken and sweetcorn soup so I decided to use the leftovers from a roast chicken dinner to produce this. It's not greatly different to the Chinese chicken and sweetcorn soup you would get from a takeaway or in a restaurant except that it is a little heavier due to the potatoes, which makes it a meal rather than a light starter soup.

"This really isn't meant to be a fixed recipe, it's more of basis to give you an idea how you can turn what a lot of people would just waste or at best compost, into a delicious meal.

"I used a pressure cooker, mainly for convenience and speed, but the same can made just using a large saucepan with a lid and more time, perhaps an hour simmering until vegetables are tender.

"So easy to make and delicious! Try adding a little grated cheese on top when serving. Lovely with some crusty homemade bread."

Serves 4 to 6

- 1 stripped medium size roasted chicken carcass
- 1 onion, finely chopped
- 2 cloves of garlic, finely chopped
- 1 tablespoon olive oil or any veg oil would do
- 6 small leftover boiled potatoes
- 1 mug of frozen sweetcorn
- 4 heaped teaspoons of cornflour
- 2 teaspoons of dried ginger or grated fresh ginger
- 3 chicken stock cubes
- 1.2 litres water

Add the onion and garlic to the heated oil in the base of the pressure cooker. Gently fry for about 5 minutes to soften and brown the onions.

Add the water and the broken up chicken carcass into the pan, turn up the heat and place the lid on. Once the cooker achieves pressure (15lb/sq in) turn down the heat to minimum to just keep it hissing gently. After 5 minutes switch off the heat and leave it to cool down so it is no longer under pressure. Pour the liquid through a sieve into another pan. Allow the contents of the sieve to cool so you can handle them without burning your fingers. Remove the chicken bones and any meat. Add the cooked onion back into the pan. Add the cooked potatoes and blitz with a hand blender in the pan.

Add the stock cubes and dried ginger and taste – it may be salty enough just from the stock cubes. Add salt and pepper as required. Add the sweetcorn and gently simmer for 5 minutes. Whilst the soup is simmering, remove any meat adhering to the bones and chop or pull apart any larger pieces of meat. Add to the soup. Mix the cornflour with a little water and add to the pan, keep stirring until it thickens. If not thick enough, add a little more cornflour.

The potatoes are optional, of course. If you had mashed potato left over that would work but I don't think roast would be quite right.

Another option we have used in the past is to add a pack of noodles to the soup to bulk it up. The soup can be frozen into portion sizes.

Pumpkin Soup

I am always surprised when people tell me they didn't realise you can eat all those pumpkins that get carved into lanterns at Halloween. Of course you can - flesh, pulp and seeds. It is all good. You can use any basic soup recipe but this one is vegan and includes making emergency stock just from onion peel, so it is very cheap and efficient.

To make a large pot of soup

- 1 tablespoon olive oil
- 5 onions
- 1 or 2 pumpkins – flesh and pulp scraped out – keep seeds for roasting
- 2½ litres of water
- a selection of herbs, such as parsley, lovage, celery leaves, fennel leaves, thyme, rosemary, any combination and amount
- cayenne pepper or chilli powder

Firstly peel and chop the onions and pop the peel and the ends into a pan large enough to hold 2½ litres of water. Add the water and bring to the boil.

While that is going on, sweat the onion in a frying pan for a few minutes and remove from the heat. Chop up your pumpkin flesh into chunks so that it cooks a bit quicker, then go foraging in your store cupboard or the garden for whatever herbs you can find.

Once your onion peel is boiling, turn down the heat and allow to simmer for about 25 to 30 minutes. Strain this into another large pan and discard the onion peel in your food waste bin or compost caddy.

Split the liquid between your two large pans and add half your fried onion to one and half to the other. Split the pumpkin chunks, pulp and herbs between the 2 pans, bring them to the boil again, then turn down to simmer. Add in the cayenne pepper or chilli powder. You might want to be cautious at first and add just a teaspoon as you can always add more.

Cook until the pumpkin is soft, which will be around 20 minutes. Stir and taste every now and then to check for spiciness and add a little more if you want to increase the heat. Remove the herbs before blitzing with a hand blender: if you mix green and orange you get brown, and I think that pumpkin soup looks nicer when it stays orange.

Taste the soup and season with salt and black pepper and a little more spice if needed. You can sprinkle some chopped herbs on the top and some people like to add a swirl of cream too.

White Sauce

White sauce is a great way to use up excess milk, even when it is on the turn and slightly sour, which is not great for in your tea and on your cereal but perfect in a sauce or in scones.

- 1 tablespoon plain flour
- 100g butter
- 500ml milk
- black pepper

In a medium saucepan, melt the butter gently and then stir in the flour, keeping stirring it over the heat for about a minute until you get a sandy texture. Remove from the heat and stir for a bit longer until it starts to look like a smooth paste. Add in a little milk and stir again until you have a smooth paste. Return to the heat, add a little more milk and stir, then add the rest of the milk, and stir for a little while. Then you can just allow it to heat up giving it an occasional stir, but keep your eye on it as it nears boiling (when you start to see bubbles). Then watch it closely. You need to let it start to come frothing up the pan and swiftly remove it from the heat as it nears the top. Grind in some black pepper and your white sauce is ready.

Cheese Sauce

Make the white sauce as described above and melt in grated or crumbled cheese and any cheese rind that you want to use up.

Custard

My Dad makes great custard using Birds Custard Powder. If we have milk to use up, I will make a crumble and Dad makes the custard.

- 500ml milk
- 2 tablespoons of Birds custard powder
- 1½ tablespoons sugar

Mix the custard powder and sugar with the minimum amount of cold milk until you get a smooth but thick paste. Boil the rest of your milk. You need to catch it at the point at which it is frothing up the side of the pan and then pour it over your paste and stir.

Sweet and Sour Balti Sauce

by Karen Cannard, The Rubbish Diet – Suffolk

Karen says: "This sauce is very easy to cook and extremely forgiving in its variation of ingredients, making it a great First Aid dish for using up leftovers in the fridge. We usually use chicken but it also works well for lamb or beef, either fresh or leftover from a roast dinner. If you prefer a veggie dish, substituting the meat with chunks of potatoes or squash works well too. It can be served with rice and anything left is fabulous for sandwiches or wraps."

These ingredients can be adjusted to suit your taste or according to the amounts are left in your fridge.

Serves 4

- 3 generous tablespoons Greek yoghurt, thick natural yoghurt or crème fraîche
- 3 tablespoons mango chutney
- 2 tablespoons tomato purée – substitute with 1 tin chopped tomatoes
- 2 cloves of garlic (crushed) – try a chopped onion as an alternative.
- 1 teaspoon chilli powder or fresh chillies
- 2 teaspoons garam masala (mixed spices, great for curries)
- a sprinkle of salt and pepper
- 1–2 tablespoons vegetable oil /corn oil
- 200ml cold water, adjust as necessary depending on whether you prefer a thin or thick sauce
- chopped coriander, to serve
- 2 teaspoons double cream or single cream

To make the sauce, add the Greek yoghurt, mango chutney and tomato purée to a small bowl and mix well. Continue to mix, adding the garlic, chilli powder, garam masala and a sprinkle of salt and pepper. Add extra according to taste.

Using a large saucepan or wok, heat the oil, bringing it to a high temperature very quickly – now's the time to add any onions, should you wish to vary the recipe – cook for a couple of minutes until soft.

Stir the sauce mixture into the oil and mix well, cooking on a high heat for 3 minutes. Gradually stir in the water to thin the sauce. Cover and leave to simmer for 5 minutes. If the sauce seems too thin, remove the lid, to let it reduce.

Use this sauce to make a delicious meal with any left over meat and veg. Add the cream and coriander just before serving.

Herb Salsa Verde

by Sara Green, Derby Food Assembly

Sara says: " This is a green sauce, which you can make as chunky or smooth as you wish. It's a great way to use up any leftover herbs or greens in the fridge, and can accompany any meat or fish dish. You can adapt it using any herbs depending on your own taste or what you are serving it with. There is no exact recipe, you can add as little or as much of each ingredient as you like, but you need to add enough olive oil to make it a sauce. You can also use a number of wild herbs such as wild garlic or sorrel."

- a handful of herbs
- 1 clove of garlic
- olive oil, as needed
- lemon juice / red wine vinegar

Chop the herbs finely and put in a medium bowl. Add each ingredient and stir in, tasting as you go – you can also add chopped capers, mustard or gherkins. Add olive oil and stir thoroughly to create a sauce-like texture.

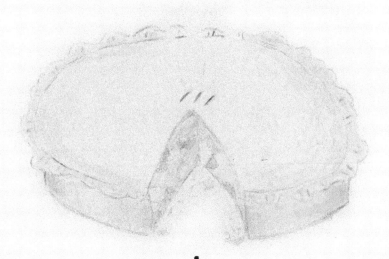

Cakes
and desserts

Cinnamon Wraps with Berry Compote and Chocolate Banana Nice Cream

by Mandy Mazliah, www.sneakyveg.com

Mandy says: "When I was asked by Mission Deli to create some recipes using wraps I knew that I wanted to make something that would solve the problem we always have of what to do with the one or two leftover wraps at the end of the packet. This is a really simple dessert recipe that can be made for yourself even if you only have one wrap left over. It's also a great way to use up any bananas you may have that are starting to go brown in the fruit bowl. And if you use a bag of frozen berries for the compote it's cost effective too."

Serves 4

For the nice cream
* 3 bananas, chopped
* 1 tablespoon raw cacao powder/cocoa powder

For the berry compote
* 400g mixed berries, fresh or frozen (I use a bag of frozen blackberries, strawberries, blackcurrants and redcurrants)
* 2 tablespoons water

For the wraps
* 2 tablespoons coconut oil
* 1 tablespoons maple syrup
* 1 teaspoons ground cinnamon
* tortilla wraps

To make the banana nice cream

The day before you want to make this, chop the bananas and pop them in the freezer. If you lay them flat on a tray for the first hour or two this will stop them from sticking together, which is kinder on your food processor.

When you're ready to make your nice cream simply put the frozen bananas in a food processor with the raw cacao powder and blend until smooth and creamy. You may need to scrape the sides down with a spatula a couple of times.

To make the berry compote

Put the fruit in a small saucepan with a lid. Add the water and heat, covered, over a low heat until the fruit has defrosted. Take the lid off once defrosted and cook for a further ten minutes. Stir occasionally.

To make the cinnamon wraps

Pre-heat the grill.

In a small frying pan heat the coconut oil, maple syrup and ground cinnamon together until the coconut oil has melted

Spread the wrap with the cinnamon mixture and place under the grill for one minute

Transfer the wrap to a plate, spoon over some of the fruit, add a dollop of ice cream, wrap up tightly, or leave flat if preferred, and serve.

Spiced Apple Cake

This is an autumn favourite I often make for pudding on a Sunday. It is good served warm with custard, but great served cold as a tea time cake too. If you don't have your own apple tree, look around for friends and neighbours who have one as so many people are delighted to give away a few apples to someone who will make use of them. I use a basic Victoria Sandwich mix and add some spices.

Take 2, 3 or 4 eggs, depending on how big a cake you would like to make and weigh them in their shells before you start. Whatever the weight of the eggs, weigh out that same quantity of butter, sugar and flour.

- butter
- sugar (I like to use brown sugar)
- self-raising flour
- eggs
- apples
- ½ teaspoon ground nutmeg or ½ teaspoon ground cinnamon
- ½ teaspoon ground cloves

Cream the butter and sugar together. I tend to melt the butter to make this easier. Beat in the eggs, one at a time, then fold in the flour.

Add in your chosen spices and mix well.

Once you have made your cake mix, peel, core and slice the apples and lay them on the bottom of the cake tin. A single layer is fine, but I do a double layer if I have enough apples.

Pour your cake mix over the apples and spread out.

Bake at 170°C/340°F/gas 3 for about an hour. I check if it is cooked by pressing the top to see if it pops back up. It should feel firm as you do this.

When cool enough to handle, turn it out onto a plate so the apple is on top.

You can use all the bits of the apple you'd normally discard to make a lovely Apple Membrillo – see Jareth Mills' recipe for this (page 167). If you don't have time to make the membrillo at the same time as the cake, then pop the apple bits into the freezer. You need quite a lot of it to make just a small amount of membrillo.

Tiramisu

This recipe is adapted from my grandmother's popular Sunday dinner dessert. I bake a lot of cake over the summer for my village cricket teas and we often have cake left that we don't finish before it dries out. Tiramisu is a perfect way to use up ageing cake.

Serves 6

- old cake – chocolate, coffee or vanilla sponge is good
- 1 coffee cup measure of Tia Maria
- 1 coffee cup measure of very strong coffee
- 1 large tub of cream cheese
- icing sugar to taste – about 3–4 tablespoons
- chocolate for grating to decorate the top (less than 1 square) or you could use chocolate sprinkles

I use one of my grandmother's pretty glass trifle dishes. 1 tub of cream cheese will cover a dish about 24cm diameter with a 1cm thickness.

Break up the cake into the bottom of the serving dish and then pour over the coffee and the Tia Maria and leave it to soak into the cake. Meanwhile, scrape the cream cheese into a mixing bowl and add in the icing sugar: you can start with a couple of table spoons, then taste it and if you like it sweeter add in another tablespoon. Repeat if you want it still sweeter.

Layer the cream cheese mixture on top of the cake mixture and then decorate with grated chocolate.

Fridge Cake

*Another cricket tea favourite. This recipe is from **101 Ways to Live Cleaner and Greener for Free**, and I have reached for my copy so many times to make fridge cake. You would think I'd know it by heart by now!*

* 300g any old chocolate that's lying around - I often use up Easter egg chocolate this way
* 100g unsalted butter
* 150g golden syrup or agave syrup
* 250g of any biscuits that need using up or broken biscuits you sometimes see in the supermarket
* 200g approximately of any kind of dried fruit

Melt the chocolate, butter and syrup. Bash up the biscuits and add them to the chocolate mixture. Stir in the dried fruit. Press in to a large loaf tin lined with cling film and leave to set in the fridge.

Bread and Butter Pudding

When my children were very little I was still doing the regular supermarket shop, and I used to keep the girls entertained while we shopped by buying a baguette and giving them some to munch on on their way round. Only once, ever, did the person on the checkout look puzzled by the remaining half baguette. We sometimes had baguette left over, so we used to make bread and butter pudding. My friend, Sue, suggested the addition of marmalade, which we love.

* dried up bread, in slices or rounds, or bread crusts: you can collect them up in a tub in the freezer if you accumulate them slowly
* butter
* marmalade
* dried fruit such as raisins, sultanas, or candied peel (see page 168)
* custard (see recipe on page 197 or use ready made)

Spread your bread slices with butter and marmalade and arrange them in an oven proof dish.

Sprinkle the dried fruit around the dish.

Pour over the custard.

Bake in the oven for 30 minutes at 180°C/350°F/gas 4.

Avocado and Raspberry Sorbet

by Zoe Morrison, www.ecothriftyliving.com

Zoe says: "This is a delicious sugar and dairy free dessert."

Serves 2

- 1 avocado
- frozen raspberries (to match the weight/ amount of avocado)

Put the avocado into your food processor (or in a beaker to blitz with a hand blender)

Next add the frozen raspberries (in a food processor it is easier to put the avocado in first, but in a beaker using a hand blender it makes the blending process easier if you add the frozen raspberries in first).

Blend them together and keep blitzing until you can't see any green bits or any bits of raspberry: it should be a smooth mixture.

Eat and enjoy!

There are lots of possible variations on this recipe. Bananas can replace avocados, and the berries could be replaced with almost any kind of fruit. You can taste the banana, whereas the avocado has a more neutral taste. It is also not essential which element of the ingredients is frozen, just as long as some of it is e.g. the banana could be frozen and the berries not, it would still work, just make sure you blitz the softer ingredients first. Chop up your bananas before freezing.

Banana Pudding

by Richard Strauss

Richard says: "This is a great way to use up a brown banana before it goes off. We love it! It's filling, very tasty and – healthy too."

Serves 1

- 1 teaspoon butter
- 1 tablespoon oats
- 1 brown banana
- whipped cream to taste

Warm the butter and stir in the oats until they smell toasted. Leave to cool while you chop the banana into pieces and put in a glass. Top the banana with the oats and slather with whipped cream.

Increase your quantities in proportion for more people or larger servings.

Serendipity Fig Rolls

Serendipity means "lucky accident". It is one of my favourite words. This recipe came about by accident, but it was delicious. I was given a jar of fig jam. It didn't quite work as jam on its own as it was just a bit too sweet. I had long wondered what I could do with it. Then I had a slice of my friend, Ülfet's, home-made fig roll, and decided to make some myself to use up the fig jam.

Ülfet's recipe was shortcrust pastry spread with fig paste (from the figs in her garden) and rolled. It was lovely.

Mine was accidentally slightly different. In a recent cook-in with Senior Daughter to try to use up the jars that had been breeding in the fridge, I somehow must have switched over the self-raising and the plain flour. They're stored in two different crock pots and I must admit I usually check I've got the right one, but must have been a little over excited at the thought of saying goodbye to another jar. I just dolloped in the flour and had nearly put in my 200g when I noticed the bag was self-raising flour not plain flour. Ah well, I decided not to worry about it and just gave it a whirl. Delicious!

Makes 6 to 8 slices

- 100g unsalted butter, cut up into small pieces
- 200g self-raising flour
- 1 tablespoon granulated sugar
- 100ml water
- 1 jar fig paste or fig jam

Rub together the butter with the self-raising flour until it looks like bread crumbs. Sprinkle in a tablespoon of granulated sugar for the texture. Bind together into a dough by adding the water about a third at a time and using a knife to gently squish together the wet pastry into the dry crumb mix.

Using a little more flour to stop the pastry from sticking to the pastry mat and the rolling pin, roll out into a rough triangle. Spread with fig jam and then roll up along the longest side.

Bake at 200°C/400°F/gas 6 for 25 to 30 minutes until the pastry is cooked. It is delicious served warm with ice cream or custard, but also lovely as a biscuit eaten cold.

Sweet Maple Banana Crumble

by Shane Jordon, plant-based chef and author,
www.foodwastephilosophy.com

Shane says: "I have chosen this recipe because I wanted to show people how they could use their ripened bananas, which look mushy and unattractive, to create a tasty easy recipe."

Makes a 24cm crumble

- 150g self-raising flour
- 60g rolled oats
- 75g butter
- maple syrup, to taste
- 1 teaspoon cinnamon
- 4 mushy bananas

Preheat the oven to 200°C/400°F/gas 6.

Put the self-raising flour, rolled oats, butter and maple syrup into a bowl and rub the mix with your fingers until it looks like breadcrumbs.

Get a deep oven proof dish and rub butter on the bottom of it.

Place half of the breadcrumb mixture at the bottom of the dish to form one layer. Add the maple syrup and cinnamon to the chopped bananas. Spread the chopped banana mix evenly on top of the breadcrumb mix. Place the remaining crumble mixture over the banana filling until it is completely covered and drizzle some maple syrup on top.

Bake for about 15 minutes, until crispy and brown. Take it out and leave to cool for 2 minutes - then it's ready to eat! Serve with ice-cream or custard.

Banana Bread

by Dean Pearce, @FoodRecycleDean

Dean says "Another family favourite is banana bread. There are loads of online recipes. I based this one on the BBC Good Food recipe called Brilliant Banana Loaf, only I don't mess around with the icing or decoration."

- 140g butter
- 140g caster sugar
- 2 large beaten eggs
- 140g self-raising flour
- 1 teaspoon of baking powder
- 2 very ripe bananas (mashed)

Pre-heat the oven to 180°C/350°F/gas 4 and butter the sides of a loaf tin and line with baking paper.

Cream the butter and caster sugar in a bowl until it's light and fluffy. Add the eggs a bit at a time, along with some of the self-raising flour and baking powder. Then fold in the remaining flour and bananas and pour the mix into the lined loaf tin. Place in the centre of the oven for 30 to 40 minutes until the loaf is nicely browned and a skewer comes out clean. It always seems to take longer than 30 minutes, so be careful to check. Leave to cool on a rack for at least 10 minutes. If I've got more bananas to use up, I'll double the quantities to make two loaves and freeze one. It's great served warm with vanilla ice cream or enjoyed cold with a nice cup of tea.

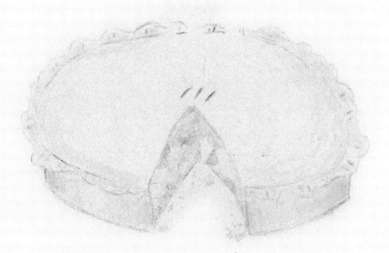

Store cupboard meals

Wacked-out Wednesday

Wacked-out Wednesday and Corned Beef Hash are my Mum's mid-week favourites. The clue is in the name. We used to put them together on a Sunday, which helps the flavours meld together by the time you put them in the oven on Wednesday. But you can also throw them together on the night. I like to use an oven proof glass dish as I like the layers of colour.

Serves 4

- 1 tin tuna
- 1 tin baked beans or chopped tomatoes
- 2 eggs
- potatoes, swede, celeriac, or sweet potato (to make enough mash to cover the top)
- butter and/or milk for the mashed potato
- salt and pepper
- grated cheddar

Peel your potatoes, swede, celeriac or sweet potato and keep the peel in the fridge or freezer to make soup or crisps when you have the time. If you steam your veg you can hard boil your eggs in the water underneath. I put the eggs into the cold water and then bring the water to the boil with the potatoes in the steamer above. Once the water is boiling you can turn down the heat.

I leave the eggs cooking for 7 to 10 minutes once the water is boiling. I then get the eggs out and put them in a bowl of cold water, while the potatoes and other veg continue to cook. Once the eggs are cool enough to handle I peel them, keeping the shells to go round my spinach in the garden to keep the slugs away. Once the potatoes and veg are cooked, mash with the milk and/or butter and season with salt and black pepper.

Put the tuna into the oven proof dish as the bottom layer, slice the eggs on top and then add the beans or tomatoes. Then cover with mash, sprinkle over the grated cheese and refrigerate until the day you want to use it, or cook in the oven at 180°C/350°F/gas 4.

Corned Beef Hash

Potatoes don't count as one of your 5-a-day but celeriac, swede and sweet potato all do. All these vegetables keep well for long periods of time in a cool, dark place, so I count them as store cupboard ingredients. By using other veg in your mash, you are getting in an extra portion of your 5-a-day.

Serves 4

- 1 tin corned beef
- 2 eggs
- carrots, grated
- potatoes, swede, or celeriac (to make enough mash to cover the top)
- butter and/or milk for the mash
- black pepper
- grated cheddar

Boil your eggs and make your mashed potato as per recipe above. While your eggs and potatoes are cooking, open a tin of corned beef, slice it and then mash it into the bottom of your oven-proof dish.

Slice the eggs on top of the corned beef and then top with the grated carrot. Corned beef is quite salty, so I don't salt my mash for this recipe. Sprinkle the grated cheddar over the top. You can then store it in the fridge for several days or cook it cook in the oven for 35 to 40 minutes at 180°C/350°F/gas 4.

I usually serve it with baked beans, or mixed beans in chilli sauce.

Pasta with Pesto

This is another of my standard store cupboard meals, often used for school lunches too. I make this for lunch when I have an unexpected day out and when I just haven't managed to prepare anything else. I can get this ready in the time it takes me to make and eat breakfast and drink a cup of tea.

- pasta, 100g per person
- pesto – you can keep a stock of jars of all different varieties, or make you own (see page 172)
- black pepper
- grated cheddar
- chopped ham or chorizo (if I have any that needs using up)

Boil the kettle, with enough water for your pasta and your cuppa. Measure out your pasta and into a large saucepan and cover with boiling water. Bring back to the boil and then simmer on a medium heat for 12 minutes. Drain, stir in your pesto and add your cheese, ham or chorizo.

Bean Casserole

Serves 4

- oil or butter (for sweating the onions if using)
- 1 onion, chopped (optional)
- 2 sticks of celery, chopped (optional)
- 1 leek, chopped (optional)
- 2 tins of chopped tomatoes
- 2 tins of any kind of beans such as borlotti, aduki, kidney beans, butter beans or 2 tins of mixed beans
- chilli flakes or chilli powder (unless your beans are already in chilli sauce)

If you are using onion, leeks and/or celery, sweat them in the oil/ butter. Once the onions are translucent, add the tinned tomatoes, and stir together, then add the beans and the chilli flakes/powder and heat everything through. Once it is all piping hot taste, season and you are ready to serve.

If you have the time let it heat gently, as that allows more of the flavours to come together. It works with or without the onion, leek and celery. If I have any I use it because I feel that adds in a bit more veg.

You can serve it with rice or with crusty bread.

Spaghetti with Chilli Oil, Sundried Tomatoes, Black Olives and Capers

This is a great pasta recipe to throw together very quickly with store cupboard ingredients. To measure out the correct amount of spaghetti, hold it in a bunch and one portion will be the size of a one penny coin. Two portions are the size of a two pence piece.

- spaghetti
- chilli oil (see page 140)
- capers
- black olives
- sundried tomatoes, chopped up a bit
- black pepper

Pop your spaghetti into boiling water, coaxing it down gently until it is fully submerged. Cook for 12 minutes. Drain your pasta, pour over the chilli oil, add in the capers, black olives and sundried tomatoes. Give a generous twist or ten of black pepper, serve and enjoy.

Sausage Casserole

I often make a double quantity of this and freeze any leftovers in single portions. I usually keep a stock of sausages from my local butcher in my freezer.

Serves 4

- 4–6 sausages
- 1 onion, chopped
- 1 leek, chopped
- 2 sticks celery, chopped
- oil or butter (for sweating the onions if using)
- 2 tins chopped tomatoes
- 1 tin butter beans or mixed beans
- chilli flakes or chilli powder (unless your beans are already in chilli sauce)

Brown the sausages. I sometimes do this under the grill, but you can do it your casserole dish. Put the sausages aside then sweat the onion, leeks and celery in the oil/butter. Once the onions are translucent, add the tinned tomatoes, and stir together, then add the beans and the chilli flakes/powder if using. Slice up your sausages and return them to the pan. You can continue to simmer on the hob or cook in the oven for about 40 minutes at 180°C/350°F/gas 4 until the sausages are thoroughly cooked.

Jacket Potato with Baked Beans and Cheese

A good, filling weekday meal, with or without a salad on the side. We sometimes have a tub of homemade coleslaw on the go which will last all week, and you can also add some pickled veg from a jar, such as pickled red cabbage, to help towards your 5 a day, but the baked beans do count. You can bake sweet potatoes instead and they do count as one of your 5-a-day, whereas somehow the potato doesn't.

- 1 large potato or sweet potato
- butter and black pepper (optional)
- ½ tin baked beans per person
- grated cheese
- coleslaw if you have any, or pickled cabbage

We usually bake our potatoes in a microwave. Heat up the beans, cut the potato in half. (Some people like to add butter and or black pepper at this stage.) Pour over the beans and then top with the grated cheese. Serve with coleslaw or pickled cabbage or a salad if you can muster one.

Pasta for a Table Full of Varied Likes and Dislikes

We have often found ourselves with a load of extra people to feed, when the daughters have friends round. With a group of 10 people to feed it is often difficult to meet everyone's varied likes and dislikes

- pasta, 100g per person, but with a large number of people you can skimp a bit usually
- 1 onion
- oil for sweating the onion
- 1 or 2 tins tomatoes
- pesto, you can keep a stock of jars of all different varieties, or make you own (see page 172)
- black pepper
- grated cheddar
- parmesan cheese
- chopped ham or chorizo
- a tin of tuna
- a tin of sweetcorn

While you are cooking your pasta, chop the onion and sweat, and then add the tinned tomatoes. This is the only bit, other than the pasta, that I serve hot. While the tomato is heating through (just needs an occasional stir), lay all the other ingredients out on the table for people to help themselves to what they like. This way you don't get people wasting stuff as they only take what they like. Anything left at the end, will go into tubs in the fridge and we will use it up for lunch the next day.

About the contributors

Alison Frith founded catering company, Artizian, in 1996, driven by a vision of delivering good cooking, nutrition and warm hospitality. Alison's straightforward ideas and philosophy – happy people, fresh natural food and attention to detail – lie at the heart of Artizian today and are why we've enjoyed continued success.

Brian Turner CBE trained at Simpson's in the Strand, The Savoy, The Beau Rivage in Lausanne and Claridge's.
In 1971 he opened the kitchens of The Capital Hotel with Richard Shepherd where they won a then rare Michelin star. In 1986 he opened his own restaurant Turner's in Walton Street, Chelsea. After fifteen years of success he opened restaurants in Birmingham and Slough and in 2003 at The Millennium Hotel in Grosvenor Square, Mayfair. Now he runs Turner's in Butlins, Bognor Regis.
Brian is the President of the Royal Academy of Culinary Arts which he has combined with a successful career as a TV personality. Having been on the first ever 'Ready Steady Cook' show, he served 14 and a half years on the very successful programme as well as many appearances on 'This Morning', 'Saturday Kitchen' etc and more recently his own show 'A Taste of Britain' on the BBC. In 2015, he recorded a new show also with the BBC, 'My Life on a Plate'.
Brian plays an active role in campaigns to encourage British people to get back into the kitchen and enjoy cooking even more.

Cara Harrison runs the lowcostliving.co.uk website. Her frugal home section gives ideas on saving money, saving energy and making better use of resources like the garden to grow your own or provide extra living space. Her frugal food section shows how to eat better for less and shares tips and frugal recipes.That doesn't mean living on cheap, unhealthy stodge. Frugal food is about tasty, healthy foods that everyone will enjoy. Cara is co-author of *Backgarden chickens and other poultry*, published by Right Way.

Carole Bamford dedicates her professional life to promoting sustainability, including organic farming; producing and selling healthier food; and promoting the survival of traditional skills and artisan craftsmanship.
Over 30 years ago, she discovered the work of organic farmers at an agricultural show, and changed the family's estates in Gloucestershire and Staffordshire to organic, traditional, sustainable farming. In the course of this, she began the acclaimed Daylesford Organic, an enlightened retail concern spanning stores and shops which are acclaimed as a model of

excellence not only in the quality of food prepared, but also in design and presentation.

Her priorities – quality and ecology – led to the development of the Bamford brand for women's wear, bath and body products.

In 2006 she was awarded an OBE for her services to child welfare, with special reference to her work for the NSPCC.

City Harvest London is London's largest food redistribution charity. Each week, they collect over 8 tonnes of surplus food from food businesses such as supermarkets, restaurants, caterers, and others, and deliver it free of charge to over 150 community projects and charities around the city for use in nutritious meals that feed some of London's most vulnerable populations. They are always looking to connect with others in the food waste reduction/rescue space so feel free to drop them a line.

www.cityharvest.co.uk; www.facebook.com/CityHarvestLondon

Cyrus Todiwala, OBE DL DBA, is Chef Patron of Cafe Spice Namaste, award-winning Pan-Indian restaurant in London, Mr Todiwala's Kitchen & The River Restaurant (in Goa) and The Park Cafe in Victoria Park East. Café Spice Namasté has held a coveted Michelin BIB Gourmand for 18 years, and they are pioneers in the UK hospitality industry's campaign for the environment and sustainability.

Café Spice Namasté holds a Green Apple Award for Environmental Best Pratice, and won the Sustainable Food Award at the 2011 City of London Sustainable Cities Awards. In 2013, they were named the Best Asian Restaurant at the prestigious Asian Business Awards. In 2014 Cyrus was the BBC Food Personality of the Year. He is a Fellow of the Royal Academy of Culinary Arts, the Craft Guild of Chefs, the Institute of Hospitality and the Master Chefs of Great Britain. He is a Founding Member of the Guild of Entrepreneurs and a Freeman of the Worshipful Company of Cooks. He is a Trustee of Learning for Life and an Ambassador of The Clink, HRH Prince Charles' The Asian Trust, The Rare Breeds Survival Trust and Patron of The British Lop Pig Society.

Dean Pearce is Business Development Manager at Specialist Waste Recycling Ltd. He is a Food Waste specialist, and co-author and former project lead of 'Vision2020: UK Roadmap to Zero Food Waste to Landfill'. Follow him on Twitter @FoodRecycleDean.

Douglas McMaster is Head Chef and owner of Silo Restaurant, Brighton. Silo promotes a pre-industrial food system as a Zero waste Restaurant. Silo was conceived from a desire to innovate the food industry whilst demonstrating respect: respect for the environment, respect for the way our food is generated and respect for the nourishment given to our bodies. Silo creates everything from its whole form cutting out food miles and over-processing whilst preserving nutrients and the integrity of the ingredients in the process. silobrighton.com

Emma Marsh MAPM FRSA was formerly head of WRAP's consumer food waste campaign, Love Food Hate Waste, which helps raise awareness of the issue of food waste in the home. Love Food Hate Waste offers simple everyday tips, recipes and advice to help people change their behaviour and waste less food. Under her leadership, WRAP helped achieve a 21% reduction in avoidable food waste in the UK between 2007 and 2012. Emma has now moved to pastures new and is currently RSPB's Regional Director for the Midlands and continues her work on and interest in food, farming and nature.

Gill Watson is a chef, food activist and writer. Prue Leith described Gill's book, *Eating My Words*, as 'sometimes farce, sometimes tragedy and all the time a foodie's handbook'. It is an account of 18 months working as a private chef to Pierce Brosnan, a supermodel and an arms dealer who shot his last chef. Gill blogs on 'Food, Family and a Few Famous Friends' at gillwatson.co.uk but more recently her blog has included personal stories of the injustices she sees every day while working with families who are struggling with poverty in Lancashire. Gill's role as a food activist, rescuing food from Lidl and FareShare was featured in the BBC film 'Inside Out' in February 2015. Find her on Facebook at facebook.com/GillWatsonBudgetCooking/.

Hannah Jacobs is Network Coordinator and co-founder at Good Food Oxford. Good Food Oxford was launched in December 2013 in order to help support the existing work of many organisations in and around the city to improve our food system, to catalyse new initiatives and collaborations, and to encourage more joined-up thinking, research and policy around food issues. In 2014 Good Food Oxford drafted its Oxford Good Food Charter, a statement of values for a better food system in Oxford. This was launched during Low Carbon Oxford Week in June. Since then over 130 organisations have signed the Charter and GFO has delivered workshops, consultancy, events and networking for its members, including a 10-day Pumpkin Festival. Read more at goodfoodoxford.org/oxford-pumpkin-festival/.

Helen McGonigal is a blogger & freelance writer, literacy workshop consultant, and author of *Mummy Makes Milk*. She blogs at spotofearth.com where she writes about her family's journey towards a more eco-friendly family life in rural County Durham. Find Helen on Facebook at facebook.com/aspotofearth/ and on Twitter @SpotofEarth.

Ian Cumming is a photographer and finalist of 'The Great British Bake Off'. He blogs at ianbakes.com, where you can find a mixture of his recipes, his travellers' tales and some insights into how he came up with some of the more bizarre bakes from GBBO.

Jareth Mills is Head Chef at The Roebuck in London. As the saying goes, 'whatever grows together, goes together'. Over the years The Roebuck has built meaningful and productive relationships with their suppliers to create a seasonally changing menu, which is both sourced locally and concentrates on sustainability. The Roebuck took part in the FoodSave pilot scheme in 2014, where its kitchen waste was monitored for 3 months for analysis and review. The result showed that the pub could be saving up to £2,324 a year. Jareth's zero-waste policy earned his pub to be shortlisted for the Best Food Waste Strategy of the Sustainable Restaurant Association Awards in 2015. In 2016 The Roebuck won the Food Made Good Award.

Jen Gale started her blog 'My Make Do and Mend Year', when her family spent a year Buying Nothing New. It was initially a method of documenting their journey, but along the way a wonderful community sprang up, and Jen knew she couldn't walk away at the end of their challenge.
They have relaxed the buy nothing new 'rules' a little now, but Jen says she learned during the year (and in the years that have followed) the power of our individual choices. "The choices we all make every day. They really do have the power to change the world. In the face of climate change, resource depletion, fast fashion and a throwaway culture, one person's actions really do count." Jen now runs a vibrant facebook group alongside her blog where people share their own 'Make Do and Mend' efforts and find support, encouragement and inspiration from Jen and from other members of the group. Read more about Jen's challenge and her ongoing journey at mymakedoandmendlife.com or join her facebook group: facebook.com/groups/AMakeDoandMendLife/.

John & Val Harrison run the allotment-garden.org website. John has written articles for *Garden News, Grow Your Own, Sunday Post, Vegetarian Living* and a number of trade publications on topics associated with 'grow your own', keeping poultry at home, preserving foods and self-sufficiency. John is the author of eight books, two with Val and one with his daughter Cara. His first book, *Vegetable Growing Month by Month* was a best selling success, closely followed by *The Essential Allotment Guide* and *Low Cost Living. Easy Jams, Chutneys and Preserves* in collaboration with Val has become a bestseller because of its straightforward, honest style. Val not only tells you what to do but also what do when things go wrong. And they do! Realising many home growers just don't know what to do to store their crops, John and Val followed this with *How to Store Your Home Grown Produce. The Complete Vegetable Grower* and *Backgarden Chickens & Other Poultry*, written with daughter Cara Harrison complete the line up. John served on the National Executive of the National Vegetable Society, a charity promoting the cultivation and showing of vegetables until recently and is a fellow of the society.

Jo Wright blogs at simplybeingmum.com, which she describes as – "one mother's personal website documenting the journey toward a family life simply done." Here you will find a collection of recipes, ideas, musings and philosophies related to families who feel a pull toward a more conscious, mindful and simpler way of life. Simply Being Mum has been featured as 'blog of the week on The Guardian Live Better page. You can find Jo on Facebook at facebook.com/SimplyBeingMum/.

Karen Burns-Booth is a free-lance food and travel writer, recipe developer and food stylist with a passion for local, seasonal ingredients. She is a member of the prestigious Guild of Food Writers and regularly contributes to a variety of print publications and online recipe sites, as well as creating bespoke recipes for numerous major brands and supermarkets in the UK and Europe. In addition to writing for her own site, lavenderandlovage.com, she also writes for Great British Chefs and runs a seasonal cookery school in south west France.

Karen Cannard is the co-founder of the award-winning Rubbish Diet, the UK's slimming club for bins, which helps households reduce their waste. She's featured on 'ITV Tonight' as the programme's Bin Doctor, has been an advisor to the BBC's 'Hugh's War on Waste' series and her behaviour change ideas have also appeared on 'Coronation Street'. Karen is also a trustee of Reuseful UK, the umbrella charity that supports Scrapstores and is a 'rubbish' columnist for local press in Suffolk. By day, she is librarian and sustainability co-ordinator for a secondary school academy in Suffolk. therubbishdiet.org.uk

Lorna Hall is the author of the blog Eat Myyy Thoughts - an eco blog focusing on food, minimalism and zero waste living. It aims to demonstrate how being a little more eco-friendly is not only good for the planet, but is also good for your wellbeing and for your wallet.

Malou Herkes is a food writer and editor, on a mission to cook, eat and enjoy good food in a more waste-free way. From preserving and foraging to saving leftovers, stretching ingredients and eating seasonally, her blog, wonkyvegblog.com is about learning from our elders – grandmothers, mothers and great home-cooks – to eat well and, ultimately, waste nothing. Malou has spent the past year travelling slowly across Europe and the Middle East to learn more about good food and how to grow, cook, eat and enjoy it in a more sustainable way. Using workaway and couchsurfing, she has stayed with families, worked on farms and helped out in kitchens along the way, to learn from incredible people who already do all of those things and more.

Prior to her year of travelling, Malou was Deputy Editor for Jamie Oliver HQ. It taught her a lot about why food and the choices we make around food are so immensely important to creating a better, healthier planet.

Mandy Mazliah blogs at sneakyveg.com. Here you'll find vegetarian family recipes that are designed to get kids eating more fruit and vegetables – especially picky eaters – and plenty of hidden vegetable recipes. Mandy found that getting her children to eat five portions of fruit and veg a day has proved to be impossible (and let's not even talk about ten a day) – sometimes they don't even manage one item of fruit or veg a day. Because of this she's resorted to hidden vegetable recipes, which she shares on her blog.

Pamela Higgins is a blogger and freelance recipe developer. You can find more of her mouth watering recipes on her blog spamellab.com #IndulgingInnocently or follow @SpamellaB on Twitter and Instagram

Rachelle Strauss is founder of Zero Waste Week – an annual awareness campaign that gets participants rethinking waste and viewing it as a resource. She was voted Winner of 'Hot 100' – *Resource Magazine's* key movers and shakers in the waste and recycling industry, has appeared in the award-winning film 'Trashed' with Jeremy Irons and once had her bin emptied live on breakfast TV! She is author of four books; all available on Amazon, and provides personal coaching to help you become the Green God / Goddess you dream of being.

Although he enjoys bashing bananas over the head and slathering them with cream, **Richard Strauss** is more at home sweating behind a computer keyboard than in front of a chopping board. You'll find him running his brilliantly named (even though he says himself) web agency - House of Strauss. He'll rustle you up a website, drizzle it with social media management and add a generous dash of SEO to help your customers find you on Google.

Relish exists to creatively connect and develop community through food cooking and culture. As a new social enterprise, based in Oxford's innovative art centre, we are a busy mobile team of passionate food loving, waste reducing enthusiasts, who include community chefs, cooks and nutritionists along with some great skilled Trustees. We engage with communities, drawing together diverse groups and individuals, to learn new skills, develop knowledge and experience in all things related to food. We are on an adventure, discovering and learning en route! Whether prince or pauper we all need to eat, food is dynamic and we see how it builds substantial bonds, brings physical satisfaction and through social and cultural interactions, nurtures friendships and nourishes the soul. This takes shape through informal cookery courses, workshops and events which incorporate nutrition, build skills in cooking from fresh, frozen and canned ingredients and celebrate cultures.

We love to engage with people from all walks of life as we create interactive opportunities, discovering how to improve our diets and enjoy the rich diversity of great social connectivity. This in turn contributes to the healthfulness of local communities.

We firmly believe that as people living in a consumer lifestyle, being wealthy does not necessarily mean being healthy. Relish delights in creating and facilitating new ideas and reviving older wise ones, using basic ingredients, brought or grown, given or foraged; cooking for optimum nutrition and wellbeing.

Our friends at the valued Oxford Food Bank generously supply us with a significant amount of fantastic fresh produce and a wonderful assortment of dry ingredients, all destined for landfill. We love the value this brings and the inspiration it gives for people to experiment with cooking Environmentally this ethos means we can make a positive environmental contribution.

Rubies in the Rubble, founder **Jenny Costa**, started reading about the problem of food waste after seeing the amount of discarded produce at fruit and veg markets across London. Beautiful mangoes, cranberries and tomatoes all headed for landfill, often because they simply didn't look right. The scale of the problem of food waste got Jenny thinking about what could be done with all this surplus produce. Surely there was a way of creating a delicious, first-class product using excess produce? Armed with some family recipes and a car-bootful of rescued fruit & veg from the New Covent Garden market, the experimentation in the kitchen began! It wasn't long before... Rubies in the Rubble hit the shelves.

Saascha Celestial-One, co-founder of Olio, The Food Sharing Revolution. OLIO is an app connecting neighbours with each other to share their surplus food and other household items. At OLIO we believe food sharing is the answer to building a more sustainable food future, one in which every person on the planet has enough to eat and we don't destroy the planet in the process. OLIO can be downloaded for free at OLIOex.com. **Sally-Jayne Wright**, food journalist and blogger, teaches food-writing in London. She gets upset when she sees untouched apples and chicken carcasses thrown out on the street. If the apple's not as crisp as you'd like, grate it into cake, muesli or porridge. Strip the meat off the carcass and make soup. A farmer grew that apple and a chicken died for you. Show respect. sally-jaynewright.co.uk

Sara Green runs Derby Food Assembly, a community-based food initiative in Derby, supporting hardworking producers and putting money back into the local economy. You can find the Derby Food Assembly on Twitter @DerbyFA. The Food Assembly is a network of online farmers markets supporting local food producers: foodassembly.com

Shane Jordan is a vegetarian chef and education practitioner from Bristol and author of Food Waste Philosophy. Apart from his interest in recycling and environmental issues, Shane specializes in creating imaginative meals from surplus food. He began cooking seriously when he was asked to prepare vegetarian cuisine for the Harbourside Market in Bristol. The success of his cooking prompted him to cook professionally in cafés, and for events and banquets throughout the South West. Shane is also using his culinary skills to cook meals for homeless shelters and raise money for charitable organizations. His interest in food waste started when he was first introduced to the registered charity FoodCycle (foodcycle.org.uk). After learning about food waste issues, Shane decided to find a way to reduce waste by creating meals from vegetable and fruit skins. From this point, Shane started to take an interest in sustainability and environmental issues, becoming knowledgeable about this subject and working with environmental groups and collaborating with local councils.

Susanne Austin is a writer, presenter & workshop host – specialising in the areas of Personal and Environmental Wellbeing – eco-build, sustainable, green and 'one planet' living as a business and daily lifestyle choice for all. She was winner of the NatWest Venus 'Green Business' Award for Oxfordshire in 2014 – In the words of another: "In a Nut Shell – She's a bit of a Divinely Guided - Earth Mother!" Grace Puskas. Susanne can be contacted via info@susanneaustin.co.uk

The Wiggly Worm is a charity that exists to improve health, well-being and self-esteem amongst the vulnerable, disadvantaged or seldom heard. Founded by Rob Rees MBE DL and managed by Abby Guilding and her team, The Wiggly Worm runs cooking clubs for young people, classes for those in independent living centres, works with food as a rehabilitation for stroke victims, mental health patients, drug and alcohol abusers as well as managing food research projects, developing awards or coaching projects. The Wiggly Worm also coordinates the #nochildhungrygloucestershire project helping to break the cycle of challenge and chaos with food.

Thomasina Miers was winner of 'BBC MasterChef' in 2005. She is a cook and food writer whose work has ranged from cheese-making and running market stalls in Ireland, cheffing with Skye Gyngell at Petersham Nurseries to co-founding the restaurant group Wahaca, winner of numerous awards from OFM's cheap eats to winner of the SRA's most sustainable restaurant group three years running. Tommi has written for the *Financial Times*, the *Times* and has a regular column in the *Guardian* magazine on Saturday. She has written and co-edited 6 cookery books (*Soup Kitchen*; *Cook*; *Wild Gourmets*; *Mexican Food Made Simple*; *Wahaca, food at home* and *Chilli Notes*) with her 7th, *Home Cook*, now out, published by Faber & Faber. She has presented various cookery TV programmes and makes regular appearances on the radio. She shops at her local market in keeping with her love of seasonal food, which she often cooks with touches of spice.

Tom Hunt is an award-winning chef, food writer, food-waste campaigner, author of *The Natural Cook* (published by Quadrille 2014) and ambassador for the Soil Association. Tom prioritises people and the environment within his work and believes in a fair global food system where our actions benefit community, biodiversity and wildlife.
Tom worked with Hugh Fearnley-Whittingstall as a course leader, cook and food stylist on the 'River Cottage' TV series. In recent years Tom has had the privilege of working alongside many of his heroes at numerous events including chefs Dan Barber, Francis Mallmann and Skye Gyngell. Tom founded Poco in 2004 as a roaming restaurant. Poco is now a seasonal tapas restaurant based in Bristol and London. Poco was awarded Sustainable Restaurant of the Year 2016. Poco follows Tom's Root to Fruit Eating philosophy, is 100% seasonal, and 95% waste free, recycling and composting everything. Tom also runs Forgotten Feast – a campaign promoting sustainable food through dining and celebration – working closely with charitable organisations Slow Food, FareShare and Action Against Hunger whilst highlighting important concerns in the food industry.

Vicky Owen is a hobby blogger, writing about homegrown and foraged food and drink, wasting less and buying less. You can find her blog, Homegrown and Foraged, at: allotmentrecipes.wordpress.com.Vicky is a member of the Zero Waste Bloggers Network zerowastebloggersnetwork.com and you can find her on Twitter @busygreenmum.

Wendy Graham writes Moral Fibres, a green lifestyle blog at moralfibres. co.uk. Wendy believes that sustainable living should be hip, not hippie. On her blog you'll find all sorts of thrifty and easy hints and tips for living a greener life that won't compromise your sense of style.

Wendy Shillam's roof top plot will be of interest to anyone wanting to grow edibles in an urban location. Situated five floors up in London W1 and five minutes from Oxford Circus, this unlikely garden makes use of raised beds with only six inches of soil. Wendy grows herbs and salad crops organically. There is a tiny greenhouse full of tomatoes and cucumbers. An elder bush, roses and Japanese wineberries protect the beds from high winds. A grapevine flowers and fruits happily above a sunny arbour. Read about it at rooftopvegplot.com.

Zoe Morrison blogs at ecothriftyliving.com and is currently writing a book – The Ecothrifty Kitchen. She is also developing online courses. Both the book and the courses will be all about saving money and the environment by reducing waste in your kitchen. Zoe runs a friendly Facebook group where members share their tips and tricks for reducing food waste as well as asking for help for what to do with those tricky leftovers. Join the group here: facebook.com/groups/reduceyourfoodwaste/. Zoe can often be found Twitter and Instagram on @ecothrifty.

Acknowledgements

A big thank you to Rae Strauss, founder of Zero Waste Week, not just for inspiring me to write this book, but for her background support and encouragement during the process of putting the book together.

Thank you to my editor Fiona Richmond for coordinating the fantastic response from peer reviewers. Thank you to all those people who gave up their time to check through my text and thank you for the support and encouragement that went with it: Anna de la Vega, founder of The Urban Worm, Dan Barber of wastED, Debra Barnacle from Agrivert, Eileen Robinson of Oxfordshire County Council, Jan Holah, Janet Witcombe and Lynda Smith, Oxfordshire Master Composters, Jeremy Jacobs of The Renewable Energy Association, Marta Owczarek of Snact, Patrick Mahon of WRAP, Saasha Celestial-One, Founder of OLIO, and Sara Green of Derby Food Assembly.

Thank you, of course, to all 40 of my wonderful contributors. You fill me with optimism for the future of food. What great work you are all doing to bring about the sustainable future that we need. I have been totally blown away by how well this book has been received by top chefs, food waste campaigners and food writers. Thank you all for sending in your recipes. Thank you to Malou Herkes for recipe editing and to Jen Pitt and Fiona Richmond for continuing the task under Malou's guidance.

Thank you to Leonie Sooke, food stylist and Kristy Noble, photographer for some wonderful images and a lesson in how to make food look great without it going to waste. Thanks too to James Wildman for more photography, as well as book design and layout, and to the contributors who also provided their own images.

Thank you to Naomi Clark for help with the book cover layout, to Evie Brass and Emma Stinchon of St Christopher's C of E High School in Accrington for the leftover pie cover image and to Wendy Litherland for making it happen, to Jenny Taylor for graphics enhancement and to Abby Manning for the apple pie image on each chapter heading. Thank you to Jo Lewington for the wormery illustration. Thank you to Nicola Saward for proofreading.

Thank you to my writing group for always being there with support, ideas, and contacts for the practical tasks that go into making up a book. Thank you to Pete Jackson, Stephanie Hale and Arvind Devalia for setting me out on the writing path.

Thank you to my family for the encouragement with this book, the practical help and the shared love of good food.

I first started to talk about this book four years ago, and since then I've discussed it with many of the wonderful people I've met in person or on social media whilst campaigning to encourage people to adopt a less wasteful lifestyle. I am very grateful for all the support and encouragement you've given as well as the tasty recipes many of you have contributed.

I've had the privilege of trying these recipes and eating the results. The wonderful food that can be made with what might have otherwise been wasted is just stunning.

To everyone who is standing with me in the fight to reduce food waste, keep going, keep cooking, keep writing and keep eating. Bon appétit!

About the author

Anna Pitt is a writer and environmental educator, specialising in waste reduction and sustainable living. She blogs about green lifestyle at: rosiesecoblog.blogspot. co.uk. She is an engaging speaker and campaigner encouraging people to look at their waste habits and promoting sustainable consumption.

Anna's first book, *101 Ways to Live Cleaner and Greener for Free*, is available online and in print. She has designed The Dustbin Diet workshop for secondary schools, which allows schools to create and sell their own version of her book. She presented the book and workshop at Best of Both Worlds 2014 – the 6th International Conference for Sustainable Development and Education. Her full paper was published in the conference proceedings. Her subsequent co-authored paper, Sharing practice from around the globe: Feedback from the Best of Both Worlds Environmental Education and Education for Sustainable Development Conference 2014 was published in Sage Journals' *Local Economy* magazine in April 2015. (lec.sagepub.com/content/30/4/452.abstract)

Anna is a Love Food Hate Waste Champion for Oxfordshire County Council and a Blog Ambassador for Zero Waste Week. She is a member of the London Environmental Educators Forum (LEEF) and an assessor for Eco Schools England. She gives regular talks and workshops in primary and secondary schools. Anna has spoken as part of the Sainsbury's #WasteLessSaveMore launch and her zero waste lifestyle has featured in *Recycleopedia.com, Oxfordshire Limited Edition, Oxford Times, Witney Gazette* and *Psychologies Magazine*. Anna formed part of a panel of experts at Oxford Brookes University's screening of 'Just Eat It'. She has been interviewed by That's Oxford TV and featured on ITV and BBC news programmes discussing food waste and formed part of a panel of experts on packaging reduction for BBC Radio Four's 'PM'. She is a regular columnist for her local magazine, *Bampton Beam*, as well as an occasional blogger for Psychologies Life Labs.

Anna has a B.A. (Hons) in Education and French from Froebel College in London, and a Master of Arts in Creative Writing and New Media from De Montfort University in Leicester. She holds the City & Guilds 7306 Further and Adult Teachers' Certificate, and a Food Hygiene Certificate. She is a Fellow of The Royal Society of Arts.

Index of recipes

Making the most of your meat 115
Chicken and Leek Pie 116
Cottage Pie 118
Shepherd's Pie 118
Bung it all in Risotto 119
Chicken and Mushroom Risotto 120
Rogan Josh 121
Sweet and Sour Pork 122
Pork Mince Marsala 124
A Pork Sandwich 124

Making the most of your vegetables 125
Vegatable Chilli with Brown Rice and Cucumber Raita 127
Broccoli Stalks with Houmous Dip 128
Braised Cauliflower Leaves 129
Potato Cakes 129
Refried Chip Shop Chips 129
Middle-Eastern Style Lentil and Cabbage 130
Leon's Pumpkin with Leeks and Sage 130
Buttered Radishes with Caraway 131
Radish Leaf Soup with Caraway 132
Cauliflower Steak, Mushroom & Lemon Thyme 134

Using up the glut from the garden and hedgerows 137
Rhubarb and Apple Jam 138
Ratatouille 140
Chilli Oil 140
Spinach or Chard with Poached Egg 141
Blackberry and Apple Crumble 141
Chutney Challenge 142
Zero Food Miles Salad 145
Nettle Pesto 146
Zingy Orange, Rosemary and Honey Infused Water 147
Elderflower and Ginger Cordial 148
Wild Garlic Bread 150

Loving your leftovers 151
Egg and Vegetable Fried Rice 152
Dead Bread Pudding 152

Panzanella Salad   154
Use-it-up Tuna, Runner Bean and Kohlrabi Lasagna   154
Pasta Bolognese Pie   155
City Harvest Super Hash   156
Wild Mushroom and Herb Arancini   158
Tomato End Salsa   159
Bubble and Squeak   159
Cornish Pasty   159
Homity Pie   160

Better use of the bits   163
Jam   164
Apple Membrillo   167
Candied Citrus Peel   168
Vegetable Peel Stock   169
Fish Stock   170
Chicken Stock   170
Chard Stem with Black Eye Beans   171
Carrot Top Pesto   172
Radish Top Pesto   172
Broccoli Stalk Gravy   173
Use-it-up Salad Dressing   173
Potato Skins with Cheese and Bacon   174
Potato Skins with Cream Cheese and Chives   174
Easy Mash Potato   174
Faggots   175
Sage and Onion Stuffing   176
Sausage Roll   176

Use-it-up snacks and light lunches   177
Olio Guac   178
Vegetable Peel Crisps   178
Spanish Omelette   180
Paneer   180
Watermelon Fois Gras   181
Cheese Toasty   181
Mango, Ginger and Cardamon Cookies   182
Blueberry, Apple and Banana Snact Energy Bars   183
Crispy Fried Salt and Pepper Banana Skins   184
Spinach Quiche   185
Parmesan Bites   186

Soups and sauces — 187

Nail Soup — 188
Frugal Green Soup — 190
Broccoli and Cheese Soup — 192
Cucumber Soup — 192
Bean Broth, Made Good — 193
Leek and Lettuce Soup — 194
Chinese Style Chicken & Sweetcorn Soup — 194
Pumpkin Soup — 196
White sauce — 197
Cheese sauce — 197
Custard — 197
Sweet and Sour Balti Sauce — 198
Herb Salsa Verde — 200

Cakes and desserts — 201

Cinnamon Wraps with Berry Compote — 202
Banana Nice Cream — 202
Spiced Apple Cake — 205
Tiramisu — 206
Fridge Cake — 207
Bread and Butter Pudding — 207
Avocado and Raspberry Sorbet — 208
Banana Pudding — 208
Serendipity Fig Roles — 209
Sweet Maple and Banana Crumble — 210
Banana Bread — 212

Store cupboard meals — 213

Wacked Out Wednesday — 214
Corned Beef Hash — 215
Pasta with Pesto — 215
Bean Casserole — 216
Spaghetti with Chilli Oil, Sun Dried Tomatoes,
Black Olives and Capers — 216
Sausage Casserole — 217
Jacket Potato with Baked Beans and Cheese — 217
Pasta for a Table-full of Varied Likes and Dislikes — 218

Lightning Source UK Ltd.
Milton Keynes UK
UKHW02f1029080118
315737UK00009B/177/P